"I didn't [...]

Caught u[...]
on the can[...]
lip. He waited a few seconds for the pain to subside.
"It's a well-kept secret."

"You'd appear more friendly if you let it out
sometimes."

He ignored the criticism. "You're welcome."

"For what?"

"Court."

She inserted four quarters and pressed the
button for her soda. "Thanks. I hope you don't
expect me to fall at your feet." When he didn't respond, Tia chuckled. "You're hilarious."

The laughter stung more than the insult. "It was a
gift."

"Then you need to start over in the first grade
and learn what a gift really is."

Frustration worked through his nervous system.
She was the reason he was here in the first place.
"I shouldn't have expected gratitude from you. You
fled custody. The judge should have thrown the
book at you."

"Who threw the book at you, Byron? What kept
you from seeing me behind bars for six months?"
Her brown eyes held him hostage. "You're in trouble because of me, aren't you?"

"No."

Her smile said she didn't believe him. "You'd
have testified against me if you'd made it in time.
But you're here. Coincidence? I don't think so. We
aren't so different."

What a Fool Believes

Carmen Green

Datina
Books

Kensington Publishing Corp.

http://www.kensingtonbooks.com

*This book is dedicated
with love to my daughter
Tina Green*

DAFINA BOOKS are published by

Kensington Publishing Corp.
850 Third Avenue
New York, NY 10022

All Kensington Titles, Imprints, and Distributed Lines are avail-
able at special quantity discounts for bulk purchases for sales
promotions, premiums, fund-raising, and educational or insti-
tutional use. Special book excerpts or customized printings can
also be created to fit specific needs. For details, write or phone
the office of the Kensington special sales manager: Kensington
Publishing Corp., 850 Third Avenue, New York, NY 10022,
attn: Special Sales Department, Phone: 1-800-221-2647.

Dafina and the Dafina logo Reg. U.S. Pat. & TM Off.

First Dafina mass market printing: August 2006
10 9 8 7 6 5 4 3 2 1

Printed in the United States of America

Chapter One

Tia Amberson dipped sourdough bread into creamy onion dip, calculated the caloric intake, and thought, *what the hell*? She didn't have a man anymore, so she didn't have to worry if she added a softer curve to her hips.

After two years, four months, and three days of her being Dante's woman, he'd chosen her birthday, Valentine's Day, to give her the "it's not you; it's me" speech.

How could he? She'd given him the best years of her twenties, had sacrificed an on-camera promotion to chief meteorologist in San Antonio for a second-string desk job in Atlanta, all to play wife—without the benefits of the position. Now her evil boss had her on a performance action plan, and Dante had changed the code to the alarm.

None of this fit into her "happily ever after" dream sequence.

She and her best friends, Rachel Washington and Megan Lewis, made a depressing group.

At nine o'clock this morning, Rachel's boyfriend,

Kyle, had packed his clothes and told Rachel he wasn't attracted to her anymore. Her job as a prison guard for Clayton County was a turnoff, and since she wasn't going to change careers, he had to go. The fact that he'd just borrowed two hundred dollars the day before didn't come up until the front door clicked closed behind him. By then, it was too late.

A frantic call passed between Rachel and Tia when Megan had beeped in, and they all got on a three-way call as Megan cried softly. Sonny had given her the heave-ho, too. It seemed that heartbreak was as free as oxygen.

Shell-shocked, they sat on the floor, around the mounted Ouija board table, in Megan's apartment, the store-bought birthday cake in honor of Tia's birthday a rushed necessity, just like this tired party.

"If I were hateful," Megan murmured, half drunk on Asti Spumante, "I'd send an e-mail to everybody at his job, telling them about the microscopic dimensions of his big Johnson." She hiccupped hard and shivered.

Rachel nudged home the hot sausage on a stick with a gulp of wine. "You were always bragging about how talented he was. Don't tell me you couldn't even see it."

"Had to wear my glasses." Megan wagged her finger. "Shoulda been called pinky Johnson."

"I knew it," Rachel hooted, always in the "I told you so" cheerleading section.

Megan licked her bottom lip, slow and reminiscent. "I didn't say he didn't know how to use what he had. But nobody needs to know that. Shit," she swore softly, tearing up. "I'm gonna get him for this."

"Go for it, sista," Rachel exclaimed. "Let him know he's been in a fight with a big dog."

Great. A radical drunk.

"He's not worth it," Tia said, proud to be the sane one of the group. It wasn't like she wasn't hurting, but an eye for an eye was a waste of time. "Revenge is just wrong."

"I'm ready to get my pound for a pound," Megan argued. "I've wasted a perfectly good six months of my life."

"Why shouldn't we have a little fun at their expense?" asked Rachel. The former wild child of the three, Rachel was the most unforgiving. "Revenge is like a box of chocolate. You always come back for more."

"What if you wanted to get back together with . . . you know?" Tia asked. "You've basically ruined your chances."

Rachel had switched to Heineken and stopped the bottle at her lips. "How can you even think about taking his cheatin' ass back?"

Tia hadn't wanted to admit that she'd hoped Dante would call and say he'd temporarily lost his mind. "I didn't say that I would."

"He gave you crabs, Tia. *And* trichomoniasis, and that was before he had the guts to dump you." Rachel rolled her eyes in that "I'm too disgusted to look at you" way. "He *tricked* your ass into believing he wasn't getting busy with a sleazy, STD-carryin' hoochie, and now all he'd have to do is wiggle his unibrow, and your infested behind would go back? I can't believe you didn't use condoms."

"We've been together over two years," Tia breathed deeply and wished she hadn't. Her stomach hurt.

"Okay, so I was naïve. I was also lucky, and I'll be fine. It's over between Dante and me. Now can we change the subject?"

"Not until you tell us what you're going to do to get back at him," Megan added.

Tia's stomach burned from anger and embarrassment, the stress of reliving Dante's words eating at her. A fiery burp blew out of her mouth, and she cringed at the sensation. The best way to get over Dante was to get on with her life. She reached for a pretzel, and Rachel snatched it. "Now what's your problem?" Tia demanded.

"Give me my pretzels and my wine. We're throwing that stupid cake in the garbage. You don't deserve to be in our pity party."

"You're being ridiculous," Tia told her, trying to maintain her classic calm.

"What are you going to do to him?" Rachel demanded.

"Nothing."

"Yes, you are," Rachel insisted.

"No, I'm not. I'm going to devote all my time to getting my career back on track."

Rachel and Megan both blinked at her.

"I knew something was up when you permed your locks and bought a purse with a name on the outside," Megan added sadly. "He's changed you."

"I'm going to be the on-air chief meteorologist soon," Tia insisted.

"Yeah, if Cruella De Vil doesn't fire you first," Rachel added sarcastically.

Rachel always kept it a little too real. She was getting on Tia's last nerve.

"I don't see why we can't just burn some pictures and call it a day," Tia reasoned.

Rachel gave Tia's shoulder a sympathetic pat. "Because it doesn't *hurt* him. I'm going to send a "please call" postcard from the AIDS testing clinic to Kyle at work."

"You need Jesus." Tia threw up her hands.

"And apparently you need an alcohol swab the next time somebody comes waving Mr. Ding-a-ling at you," Rachel quipped.

Tia didn't join in their laughter. "Do what you want," she told them. "But don't come crawling to me, talking about how sorry you are that Kyle got fired. You've broken up before. One day you might forgive him, and then you'll be sorry."

Megan's head dipped. "Sonny won't be back. He married his fling tonight in Vegas. They had a live video feed at lunch in the break room."

The flatly delivered dose of reality stopped them. Tia took the high road even though she wouldn't have minded seeing Sonny get eaten alive by crows. "I'm so sorry."

She kept telling herself to forget Dante, but like a pendulum, her mind swung back to the parting statement from his unemployed chapped lips. *"You got played."*

Her stomach fired up, like a boiler room full of coal. Uneasiness overtook her, and she moved around, fighting for a comfortable position. She slid up on her knees and stretched, but couldn't escape the heat his words unleashed. He'd been so cruel that she thought of little else, except to try to forget it all happened.

But she was Tia, the calm one. The one raised to

be a lady, first and last. "Let him go," Tia said, warning herself to take her own advice.

"I'm not buying it," Rachel prodded. "You have to do something, Tia. *Say something.*"

"Is that what it'll take for you to leave me alone?" Both nodded.

"OK, fine. I feel like shit," she said evenly, raising up on her knees. "When I sat in Dr. Penn's office two weeks ago, I was mortified that he thought I wasn't a good girl. After the crab/trich diagnosis, I had to get medicine, so in walks this fine male nurse to give me instructions on how to use the crab remover. Did you know there's a tiny comb in the box?"

When her friends didn't move, Tia gulped, feeling feverish. "And if that wasn't humiliating enough, Mr. Nurseman leaned down and told me to save myself the trouble and cut it all off. He even offered to help me. Crap!" The word exploded from her mouth, and she burped. Loud and long.

Megan fell back on her floor pillow, snorting. Rachel's mouth hung open wide enough to house a fly convention.

"I promise you, it wasn't funny." Tia wiped her forehead. "I stupidly asked him, 'Who does that?' Do you know what he said?"

"No." Rachel bit her bottom lip and shut her right eye to keep from laughing.

"He said, 'Who doesn't?'"

A telepathic message slid between Rachel and Megan.

Not for the first time in her life, Tia felt like she was the only one in the section labeled "last to know."

"You shave it . . . *all*?" she whispered in disbelief.

"Yep," Rachel said.

"It's cooler in the summer," Megan reasoned.

"Well, hell." Tia wasn't sure she knew her friends. Sure, she edged up her lawn. Cutting it *all* off had never occurred to her.

For this lack of knowledge, Tia placed the blame squarely on her mother's shoulders. Millicent had once told her bikini panties started the sinful sexual revolution. Although Tia knew now that wasn't true, her drawer was full of 100 hundred percent cotton thigh huggers. The one thong she owned was stuffed in the back of the drawer, in a Baggie.

But now that her friends had confessed, she wondered what else she didn't know.

"Kyle and I were straight-up freaks," Rachel offered. "He cut mine and considered it foreplay."

Tia slapped her hands over her ears. Too much information. "I've got to go. My head is about to burst." She burped and cringed. She needed antacid the size of a basketball to cool her hyper tummy.

"Will you call if you want us to send an e-mail about Dante?" Rachel asked.

"Are you determined to do it?" Tia asked.

"You bet your sweet ass we are. It's our civic duty," Megan proclaimed. "Wait a second." She weaved up the hall, with her hand out, and wrestled a gift bag from the closet. "Happy birthday."

Finally, a bright spot in her otherwise dreadful day. Tia tore off a sliver of paper and saw the knives she'd been wanting forever. "These are just like the ones from TV."

"They *are* from TV. Ginsu," Megan hiccupped.

Tia grinned. Now she'd be able to contribute to Thanksgiving in a productive way. Last year's overdone candied yams were still the joke of family get-togethers. "I'll be the hit of the holidays. Thank you."

"You're welcome." Megan's brow lifted. "Last chance to send an e-mail."

"No." Tia fastened her leather jacket and headed to the door. "You two have fun."

Tia drove her Honda Accord down the wet streets and acknowledged the irresistible urge to confront Dante. Then she'd tell him off, kick him out of her condo, and have the solid stamp of closure she needed to move on. But she wasn't confrontational. She wasn't mean, and she wasn't going over there.

Crisscrossing streets for ten minutes, she made a right on Lenox Road, and was outside their condo, the tail end of Dante's vehicle mooning her.

By rote, she steered her car toward the second parking space and slammed on the brakes.

There was a car in her spot.

Up one floor, flickering candlelight from their bedroom mocked her.

A woman was under her duvet!

While she'd temporarily moved into a hotel to give him time to sort out his feelings, he'd moved in her replacement.

She was played.

Spotting a vacant space down the next row, she drove over, slid the gearshift into park, and groped for her cell phone. If she couldn't have him, she at least wanted her five-hundred-dollar blanket back.

Tia wondered if the woman knew he had trich.

Reality thumped her on the forehead.

Maybe he'd gotten it from her, and that's how Tia'd ended up with it.

Stomach acid crawled up her esophagus, and she

groped for an antacid, then remembered they were in the kitchen drawer, along with the super-large condoms. Who had she been kidding? He'd have to fit his pinky Johnson *and* his ego into the latex in order for it to even pucker.

A hysterical laugh burst out.

This was all the fault of married women, the liars. They'd been shoveling the "we're so in love; marriage is wonderful" crap at single women since the beginning of time. She and Dante hadn't even skipped up the aisle before he'd blasted that lie into the stratosphere.

Well, she wasn't going to take it like a lady.

She reached into the backseat, grabbed one of her brand-new knives, and went to Dante's Lexus convertible.

The car was his.

She positioned the knife.

But the tires were hers.

She took a long, cleansing breath and plunged.

Chapter Two

The fourth tire on the Lexus deflated, and Tia began to shake. Revenge was exhausting.

She tried not to scratch her bald vagina and wondered how Rachel and Megan could stand not having hair down there.

They were freaks, and she wasn't.

But she was pissed off.

Tia used the end of the knife and scratched A S S-H O L E into the shiny black finish. Her work here was done.

As she moved toward her car, her adrenaline high evaporated, and sanity moved in. This was crazy.

At this point in her life, she should have had enough faith that God had a foolproof punishment plan to deal with male infidels. But God was taking His time, and as far as she was concerned, unless Dante broke out in a head-to-foot case of psoriasis, He might not mind her help this one time.

In the darkness, she tried to appear casual as she looked for her midnight blue Accord as a vehicle crept around the corner and moved up slowly on her left side.

Tia's mouth dried. Maybe slashing the tires hadn't been such a good idea, considering she had the potential of getting mugged, caught, or worse.

She walked faster as the cruising vehicle veered toward her, and the window went down.

Her mind screamed, *Duck! Drive by!* and she dropped everything, preparing for a nosedive, when searing pain shot through her foot.

It took all of a second for the cop to spot her handiwork.

"Did you do that?" he asked indignantly.

Pain made her grunt, and she quickly concluded two things.

One, she didn't want to go to jail. And, two, when caught in the act of committing a crime, never abandon the tools of the trade recklessly.

"Is that your car?"

"No, but those are my tires."

"Tomato. Tomahto. Turn around and put your hands behind your head."

"I'm allergic to penicillin."

"So?"

The harsh cruiser lights flickered over the officer's stern face. He approached with his billy club in the cocked and ready position.

"After you arrest me, I'll need stitches."

"If you don't give me any trouble, you won't have to worry about that. Now turn around. You're under arrest."

Tia lifted her knife-embedded foot and completed a quarter turn before she fainted into the officer's chest.

Chapter Three

Officer Byron Rivers waited outside the ER exam room while his prisoner sat inside, getting her foot stitched.

His mouth stayed tense with attitude, and he regretted this entire night.

Regretted reporting to work.

Regretted patrolling the condo parking lot.

Regretted catching the woman vandalizing.

He just wanted to go home. The Lakers were playing tonight.

His biggest regret was not setting TiVo to record the game. He'd been so sure he'd be home by tip-off.

Damn.

This lady was in a lot of trouble, but he couldn't help but complete his list of regrets.

He regretted scaring her so badly that she dropped the knife that gashed her foot, which caused her to faint, which made him think she was hitting on him, which made him elbow her in the eye, which made her injuries worse than they should have been.

Why had he thought her capable of such a lame ploy?

Because she was a woman, and women were the masters at playing the sympathy symphony.

Okay. He'd made an honest mistake.

But no one would see it that way. This was the second time in thirty days that one of his prisoners had been on the receiving end of his reflexes, and his new captain would have something to say about that.

The rest of the events ran play by play through his mind.

When she'd fainted, he'd swept her up against his chest.

Her breasts rose and fell in a smooth, slow rhythm. He'd held her there, his first aid training gone, before reality slapped him into the present, and he'd called for an ambulance.

He'd perched her atop the hood, his thigh at the center of her body, his left hand across her midriff.

In warmer temperatures, under different circumstances, he could conceive of them on a journey to intimacy. But the situation wasn't ever going to be like that.

This lady was a woman scorned, and she was going to jail.

He was in trouble, too, but that didn't matter right now.

He nudged the exam room door open and stuck his head inside. "How're things coming along?"

"We'll be a while," Dr. Khan said, bent over the woman's foot.

"You in a rush to blacken my other eye?" the woman asked.

Chocolate. Her right eye, her good eye, was a

delicious-looking chocolate. Byron tried to speak quietly. "I already apologized for elbowing you."

"I don't see how you could think I was going to do something to you, you big baby!" Tia tried to cover her mouth, but her handcuffed wrist stopped her.

Her gaze darted from her arm to him, and he shuffled his feet. She was about to blow.

"You have a right to be angry." He knew those were the wrong words before they'd completely fallen from his mouth.

"You bet I do," she yelled. "These cuffs are for total humiliation, right? I guess I'll hop on my one good foot, with my one good eye to guide me, and make a break for it." She shook her head, disgusted.

"I'm just doing my job."

"Yeah, well, you're superior at it. Feel better?"

An internal war waged. He'd get in big trouble if anyone found out, but she was pretty much incapacitated.

"I'm taking these off because"—*I'm a sucker*, he thought but didn't say it—"you should be more comfortable." The toe of his shoe rammed the bottom of the steel bed frame. Noise reverberated upward, and annoyance flashed across her pretty face.

Guilt be damned. She hated him. Snatching his pad from his pocket, he clicked his Bic and noticed that she'd put her hospital gown on backward.

Officer Rivers did the unthinkable.

He peeked.

She jerked the gown closed.

"I wasn't looking at your bra," he snapped.

"Right, and my eye is black because *I ran* into your elbow."

"You *did* fall into me."

"Because I was stabbed," she told him, as if he were the biggest knucklehead in the world.

Dr. Khan, who'd kept quiet, patted the woman's arm, sharing a bond. "Now, now. You mustn't get worked up again."

"Dr. Khan, I've never been worked up in my life." She breathed hard and fanned herself. "But I've had it with men who don't take responsibility for their actions. Frankly, it feels good to say exactly what's on my mind. Now beat it, Pinko," she snarled at Byron. "I'll be ready for jail when I get done."

Barracuda woman had returned.

"I was going to go easy on you—"

"Right. I just got my two front teeth capped. Want to knock them down my throat with your big stick?"

The doctor burst out laughing.

Byron walked into the hallway and slammed the door.

It popped open. He slammed it again and stalked to the coffee machine, where he shoved in quarters.

Women were nothing but trouble. He knew first-hand. He had four sisters, and they were the source of enough aggravation to choke a horse.

Where were the women of the fifties? Sweet, nice women who enjoyed being women? Every day he met women who fought, cursed, and handled themselves like mini men. He didn't get it. And then, there were the psychos.

Angry lady down the hall would get what she deserved when she went to jail.

He drank his coffee, then spit the searing liquid back into the cup. Man! This woman was pissing him off. It would be his pleasure to process her into jail. Vandalism wasn't a felony, so she'd be in holding until she made bail, but that would be enough to diffuse her mean streak.

Back at the exam room, Byron raised his pad and stared at the blank sheet. *Damn.* He still didn't have her name.

"You wrote on his car?" he heard Dr. Khan ask the woman.

"Yes."

"And slashed his tires?"

"He gave me crabs and trich. And he still has my new duvet."

Byron frowned, his judgment shifting, although he told it not to. Truth was, the creep deserved to get his car redecorated. But that didn't negate the fact that her actions were still against the law.

"Good for you," the doc said. "This is going to hurt, but once it's numb, I'll stitch you up, and you can go home . . . on your way."

"To jail," the woman corrected, sounding teary.

Here come the waterworks. Good. She'd brought this on herself. He steeled himself against his main weakness.

"Ow. Ow. Ow. Cripes, that hurts," she wailed.

"It's not Rivers's fault, you know," Dr. Khan told her.

"Don't defend *Officer Enthusiastic.* He should have asked me why I was there. Youch! How many of those blasted things do I need?"

"Shoe minimized the damage. Thirteen, maybe fifteen."

"Do you think he'll take me directly to jail?" Byron's heart tripped over the vulnerable question.

"Definitely. He's a real stickler."

"So you've dealt with him before?"

"His detainees. Six weeks ago, then again last month."

"Boy, do I feel lucky," she said, half crying now. "My ex gave me a communicable insect, and my arresting officer gets frequent visitor points when he brings a prisoner to the ER. This sucks."

Byron didn't want to agree, but what could he say? Her eye was wearing his elbow print.

"Why don't you rest, and I'll finish up? You'll be home in no time."

"Yeah, after I spend the night in jail with a butch named Alice. Oh, God. I can't believe this is happening," she sobbed. "My stomach is burning like crazy. Can I get some antacid?"

"Sure."

Dr. Khan got her history and then called a nurse. Byron stepped aside as her request was delivered.

Great. She probably had a bleeding ulcer she hadn't known about before tonight. Byron threw his head back, his mind closing the door on the hope that he'd catch the last quarter of the game.

Dr. Khan chuckled. "I'll give you a mild painkiller, and you should sleep fine."

"It's not the sleeping I'm worried about. It's the *where* that scares me."

"When you come see me in a week, you'll feel differently. Have you ever taken an anger management class?" Doctor Khan spoke with deceptive casualness.

"No. Why?"

"You're still angry."

"*I* didn't cheat on *me*. So why should I go to some class?"

"Your ex is guilty of being a bad man, yet it is you who is under arrest. This is your first offense, right?"

"I've never done anything like this before. I guess I just snapped."

"Last stitch," Dr. Khan said softly. "We'll get you situated with some crutches and a prescription."

"Do you have samples? I don't think I'll have access to the drive-through pharmacy on my way to the county lockup."

Dr. Khan made soothing noises to the weeping woman. "No problem. Come to my office in one week for your checkup. The nurse will get you a new top. Yours was ruined."

He'd used the cotton top to stanch the flow of blood, but would she believe him if he told her?

Byron couldn't help but wonder what she was thinking. He was thinking he was a schmuck, no different from the vandalized former boyfriend.

"I'll be back in a moment." Dr. Khan stepped into the hallway and pulled Byron into the exam room two doors down.

The East Indian woman gave him a smile, her dark eyes accentuated by stylish black glasses frames. "She's had a rough night," Dr. Khan began. "She needs to rest and stay off that foot. Now we can do this one of two ways. You can give her a ticket and see her home, or I can admit her to the hospital."

"There's nothing wrong with her."

"Her blood pressure is up. Or something like that," she said slyly.

"Come on, Khan, I can't just let her go."

The doctor shrugged, unmoved. "What she did was better than what could have happened to him in my country."

"I thought the women were all subservient in India." Byron bit his tongue and tasted the bitter juice of badly chosen words. "Forget I said that."

"Certainly. I'm not excusing her behavior, just saying that she needs a break. Work with me?"

"Fine." He threw up his hands and shook his head. "What's her full name? I'll give her a ticket and see her in court."

"First is Tia. Didn't get the last one. It's on the chart. Thanks, Rivers. I owe you one."

They walked back to the exam room and went inside. The bed was empty, the gown discarded. Both reached for the chart and stared at the empty door folder.

Dr. Khan looked up at him, a mysterious smile on her face. "I guess I underestimated her."

Damn. He wouldn't even catch the game highlights on ESPN.

Byron headed for the exit. "She won't get away with this."

Chapter Four

Tia awoke in the strange hotel bed, flat on her back.

Blood thrummed to her heel.

Her life was as beautiful as a train wreck.

After cleaning up and swallowing pain pills with a four-dollar oatmeal energy bar from the minibar, she considered her options.

She could skip work and save the explanation about her impaired state to Chance, her boss.

Or she could give Chance the last reason she needed to fire her.

Tia hated the position she was in. Dante had convinced her to dream big—with him in the picture. And now she was without him and almost out of a job.

Reaching for her keys triggered an instantaneous migraine.

Her car was still at the condo.

Panicking that she might actually lose her job, she hopped to the bed and dialed. "Rachel," she said when the machine beeped, "pick up."

Thirty painful seconds passed before Rachel fumbled the phone. "Hey, girl. What's up?"

"I need a huge favor."

"Right now? I'm kind of"—she hesitated, talking to someone—"in the middle of something."

Why did she sound so sleepy? And satisfied? "You've got company."

"Bingo. Bye-bye."

"Is it Kyle? I thought you two had broken up?"

"We renegotiated the terms of our relationship at about midnight, and I exercised my rights until six a.m."

Tia couldn't believe her ears. Rachel had wanted to send a "please call" AIDS postcard to Kyle just a few hours ago.

She'd remind her about that on the way to get her car. "I need a ride," Tia said.

"Where's your car?"

"Don't ask. Can you help me?"

"Tia, what's the matter? Where's your car?"

"Look, meet me outside the Marriott in Buckhead in fifteen minutes. I'll explain on the way."

"If you're going to tell you me slept with that nasty slug," Rachel said, her voice filled with reproach, "you may as well start walking."

Tia grabbed her purse. "Let's just say, I'm having a hard time maneuvering on my crutches."

"On my way."

Tia scrambled to pack and call for a bellboy. On her way in last night, she'd seen a gift shop, and there'd been a straw hat in the window. She didn't think she'd been seen at the condo, but the disguise would throw off anyone who might think she looked familiar.

***

Byron sat in the daily update meeting, scowling at what he knew was the beginning of a bad day.

Captain Chip Hanks circled the square room, belittling officers for one minor infraction or another. He'd come onboard two weeks ago, with the mindset that he was cleaning up retired Captain Ryan's mess. Hanks had destroyed the morale of what had been a close-knit unit of good officers. So far, three had already put in for transfers.

"What about you, boy wonder?" he said to Byron. "I have an arrest report." Hanks turned an innocent eye to the rest of the squad. "But no prisoner," he yelled like a Baptist minister. "We're all interested to know how a 140-pound woman with a gashed foot managed to elude her arresting officer. Slip out of the hospital and off into the night. Why don't we start with her name? What is it again? I seem to have missed it on the report."

"It's not on there."

"And why is that?"

"Because I didn't get it. I was too busy calling for an ambulance. I didn't want a dead prisoner."

"But you took the no prisoner option, right? Funny, that box seems to have been eliminated from the form."

"The doctor asked to consult with me, and while we were talking, the prisoner slipped away. I screwed up," he said. "But the last thing I or any of these other officers needs is a condescending boss who thinks belittling us is a substitute for being a good captain."

"Oh," Hanks hooted. "If I were you, I'd shut my mouth. You didn't learn much under Ryan, did you?"

Byron stood straight. "You're not good enough to breathe the same air as Captain Ryan."

"You're skating on very thin ice."

Byron shrugged. "Not worried about the temperature of the water. You?"

"In my office, now!"

"I can't believe you trashed Dante's car." Rachel glared at Tia disapprovingly. "That's so unlike you."

"Last night you two were pushing me to beat a brother down. Besides, what about you, Ms. postcard-slinging nut bag?"

"*I* can get crazy. We never expected you to."

That was nice to know now. "Stop worrying. I'm not a psycho stalking my ex-boyfriend. This was my one and only act of retaliation. What's up with you and Kyle?"

"Girl, making up is better than breaking up."

"Sick."

"Yeah," Rachel agreed. "I know."

They cruised the lot, heading toward the scene of the crime, as Tia kept a steady eye out the window. The last thing she wanted was for Dante to see her retrieving her car after what she'd done to his.

"So," Rachel said hesitantly, "how long have you been in the hotel?"

Tia's stomach bubbled awake. "Two days. We were giving each other space."

"Didn't you buy the condo?"

"I bought it from the bank. His credit was crap after they foreclosed."

"So why is he there and you're at a hotel?"

"I couldn't kick him out, Rachel. He lived there for two years before we got together. Besides, I thought we'd get back together. Obviously, last night's developments change everything."

"I'm taking it by the suitcases, you checked out."

"Right."

"Where you gonna stay?"

"That's the million-dollar question," Tia murmured under her breath. She didn't have the money to continue staying at the hotel. Closing on the condo had depleted her sparse funds—along with her recent shopping trip to Neimen's to celebrate her birthday and being a new home owner.

And Tia didn't want to ask Rachel to take her in. They'd been friends for ten years, but Rachel could get flaky. Sometimes she spoke, and sometimes she didn't. Sometimes she wanted to hang out, and sometimes she went into a cave and didn't come out for weeks. Then she'd return to the friendship as if nothing happened.

But Tia looked at Rachel and Megan as the sisters she didn't have. When she wanted them, she didn't want them to be in self-imposed exile.

Her brain scrambled as she struggled to find a good excuse not to ask Rachel.

"Megan won't mind if I crash with her for a bit, until this mess is straightened out. She's closer to the job, too."

"She'll mind, Tia."

"What the hell for?"

"She's in a bad place mentally."

"We all are—"

"With Sonny getting married on her like that, she's taking it hard."

"I can certainly understand that—"

"And she's having her apartment remodeled. She decided to buy out the owner."

Oh. Hell. "When did that happen?"

"Last night, after you left. The owner had been after her for a while. When she called him, he agreed to her counteroffer. The remodeling, which he's paying for, starts tomorrow."

"So what's up with you and Kyle?"

"We're going to take things slow. I'm not into a commitment mind-set anymore."

Since when? Tia wanted to ask but didn't. She had her own relationship issues. She could focus only on one set of problems at a time. She still needed a place to stay. "Maybe I could bunk with you for a day or two," she said quietly.

"No problem."

Even as Rachel said the words, Tia couldn't help but think she'd just made a big mistake. But she'd have a roof over her head. Then things would be straightened out. They had to be.

"How did you get to the hospital?" Rachel asked, interrupting Tia's musings.

"A-a man came along and . . . and he made an offer I couldn't refuse. Over there."

Rachel stopped the car and hurried to get out.

"I can manage from here, Rach. Thanks. I'll need a key to your place."

Her often-opinionated friend walked to the rear passenger door. "Don't worry about that. I'll be home every night by the time you get off."

Tia's eyebrows creased, but she didn't speak. *Just*

a couple days. She tried to roll out of the tiny Miata. "Rachel, I'll get the crutches."

Rachel held them back, staring at her. "You can't drag them *and* you out of the car, so quit. You act like the cops are hunting you down." Rachel looked at Dante's car and whistled. "Girl, you really did snap."

Tia glanced but didn't focus. Daylight showcased the work of a truly angry woman. She was over him now. She hobbled to her car, her hands shaking. Calling in sick looked appealing.

"Tia, I think you need to talk to somebody."

"Rach, not you, too. There's nothing to worry about."

Spice and sandlewood blended together, stirring distant memories.

"Good morning, *Tia*," the familiar male voice said, one that had played chase with her in her dreams. "We had a date last night. You got away before I could ask you out again."

Tia's stomach sank to the bottom of her sore foot. "Go away. You're not my type," she told the officer.

"Tia!" Rachel screeched. "You're never rude."

"I am when I'm getting arrested."

Rachel started gurgling as the plainclothes officer pulled out handcuffs. "I guess that's my opening," he said. "You have the right to remain silent. . . . And this time, you won't get away."

Chapter Five

The black eyes of the American eagle emblazoned on the symbol of justice stared down at Byron, as if holding him in contempt. He'd never seen the inside of the hearing room before and didn't know how officers who'd had complaints lodged against them numerous times could stand it.

Even at six-three, 220 pounds, and thirty-one years of age, he was totally intimidated.

The official surroundings stopped time and crystallized his purpose for being there. He'd been insubordinate. That much was true. With provocation. But would his explanation ever be heard? His career was on the line. Everything he'd achieved in the past five years was in jeopardy.

He and his union representative, Mabrey Jackson, sat on one side of the room, and Captain Hanks on the other, and in the ensuing silence, Byron tried to pinpoint, not for the first time, where he'd gone wrong.

He concentrated hard, not wanting to let the side

of himself that rejected everything he didn't believe in take over.

Had things started going wrong when he'd met Tia Amberson two weeks ago?

No, long before that. A year to be exact.

The day, month, and time returned.

His life had been irrevocably changed when he'd collided with LaPrincess Quinellis.

She'd run, literally headfirst, into his cruiser, bloodied and broken by the fists of the man she'd vowed to love forever. She'd been a mess physically. Battered beyond that of even a worst enemy.

He'd thought it fate that she'd rammed his cruiser with her body and he'd gotten to her before her husband. He'd saved her that night and had taken great pleasure in getting two hits in before strapping the cuffs on her husband.

That night he'd surpassed professional detachment and had allowed himself to feel. He'd sat at the hospital with the skittish woman long after his shift was over and had lectured her on the responsibility she had to save her life.

Between getting her broken nose taped and her lacerations sutured, she'd said the right words and promised to love herself more than she loved Gerald.

Byron had left that night, his purpose in life suddenly defined with crystal clarity. His job was to protect and serve.

That night he'd slept well.

Two days later he'd gotten the call at the beginning of his shift. Gerald Quinellis had killed LaPrincess the night before, while Byron dreamed the night away.

As far as Byron was concerned, LaPrincess had

played him, strummed his sympathetic emotions, and had died, anyway.

Tia Amberson wouldn't be any different. He'd saved her, and she was probably at that very moment in the arms of the man who'd dogged her.

He looked at the eagle's eyes. He wouldn't be a fool again.

Mabrey leaned toward him. "No outbursts. Don't speak directly to the captain. Let me answer the questions, unless you're otherwise asked. If you get fired"—Mabrey shrugged—"you won't get back in."

Byron considered his other occupational possibilities. Maybe he could go back to the potato chip company as a delivery driver. Not really what he had in mind.

"Captain Hanks was wrong," Byron said.

"That unrepentant attitude will ensure unemployment."

The three-member panel walked in, and everyone stood until the panel was seated.

"Officer Rivers," Colonel Tulane said, "you've been charged with insubordination to your superior officer. Do you understand this charge?"

"Yes, sir."

"Are there questions from the panel?"

Dr. Valencia Cole moved first. "Officer Rivers, please explain the details of the incident."

"On the night of February fourteenth, I attempted to arrest a suspect for vandalism. In the process of the arrest, the suspect became injured." He cleared his throat. "I thought the suspect was making an aggressive move against me, and I defended myself."

"You gave her a black eye?" Colonel Berger gave him an astounded look.

Byron pressed ahead. "The suspect was taken to Grady Hospital. During the course of treatment, I was called into a consultation with her doctor. While we were meeting, the suspect fled."

"Fled?" Colonel Berger questioned. "Fifteen stitches in the foot. Is that correct?"

This wasn't going well, and Mabrey had yet to say a word.

"Yes, sir," Byron answered.

"How was that possible? I'm assuming she was on crutches."

"Correct."

"A full investigation was performed and it looked as if the suspect fled, unaided."

Captain Hanks scoffed. "That would never happen to an officer who followed the procedure for the apprehension of a suspect. Officer Rivers is not ready to return to patrol. Furthermore—"

Dr. Cole banged her pen sharply on the table. "Please give Officer Rivers a chance to complete his statement, Captain. Thank you." She pressed on, clear as to who was in charge.

"The suspect was apprehended the following day without incident," Byron concluded.

Dr. Cole's neatly arched black brows lifted and stood out in stark contrast to her milky complexion. Her gray gaze rested on him. "Would you like to add anything else?"

Byron entertained the notion of telling his boss where he could go, but that was how he'd gotten here in the first place.

"The next day I was reprimanded during roll call, as were other officers."

"That wasn't a reprimand." Hanks pushed up

straight in his chair, getting louder. "I demanded an explanation. I have no tolerance for renegades."

"Captain." Colonel Tulane's stern tone forced the room into a stiff silence. "I've heard enough to render a decision."

Byron and the still silent Mabrey stood.

"Officer Rivers, you are required to attend sixty hours of anger management classes and are suspended for three days for failure to follow the proper arrest procedures. The other charges are dropped."

"Yes, sir! Sir?"

Colonel Berger looked up. No one dared speak after a decision had been rendered. "Yes, Officer?"

"I'm scheduled to testify at 1600 hundred hours on the case associated with this incident."

"It's 1630 now."

"Yes, sir."

"Were you the only officer to respond on that case?"

"Yes, sir."

Colonel Berger regarded him. "The suspension will begin immediately following that hearing, and I don't care if there's a riot outside the capitol. You are not to respond. Clear?"

"Yes, sir!"

"Pick up the information regarding the class at Dr. Cole's office. You are dismissed."

"Thank you, sirs. Ma'am."

"This is an atrocity," Hanks bellowed. "That officer was insubordinate, and he should be terminated."

"Captain Hanks." The colonel's voice felt like a cool steel pipe to a warm hand. "In light of your reaction to Officer Rivers and the rest of your squad, we have some real concerns about your abuse of power. Call your representative. You are officially under investigation."

Byron heard Hanks yell, "What?" then start sputtering. Good. Maybe he'd shut up for a minute.

One glance at his watch and Byron moved just short of a trot. He had three buildings and four floors to cross in order to testify in Tia Amberson's case.

He started to jog.

After what he'd been through, she wasn't going to get off easy. Not by a long shot.

Chapter Six

"Why can't we go inside?"

Outside of courtroom A, Tia stood with her second cousin and attorney, Leroy Muller. Thrice divorced because of his wandering eye, he ignored Tia in favor of the butt of a healthy, bright-skinned woman.

Tia squeezed his wrist, fingernails first.

"Ouch!" His confused gaze flew to her. "What'd you do that for?"

"I'm about to have my day in court. Can you please focus? What's the holdup?"

"They're not ready."

Inadequate, but an answer. She hoped she didn't regret throwing her business to a relative. "What's going to happen?"

"When you go before the judge, he'll read the charges. The ADA will state the recommendation we worked out, you'll waive your right to a trial, you're sentenced, then we leave."

So why am I paying you? she wondered but tried to

squelch that evil spirit. Lately, everything got under her skin. *A by-product of being cheated on,* she supposed.

Leroy's eyes flew to a woman with forty-plus breasts and a thirty-something waist. Tia forgave him. Everybody looked.

"Damn, did you see that?" he asked, as if another woman's boobs would make her brain turn to mush. His lack of tact lit the fuse in her stomach.

She snapped her fingers in front of his eyes. "Has the reason I'm here escaped you?"

"Man! You sure have changed." Leroy voiced his contempt with a frown. "You used to be nice. What happened?"

Trich. Crabs. Arrest. Bail. Hospital bill. Court. Possible compensation to Dante. Leroy had dropped that bombshell on her yesterday afternoon.

She was already out of a fortune, and her temporary lapse of sanity had changed what would have been a simple breakup into her not being able to get into the condo. But worse, she couldn't force Dante out.

The sheer irony was that she was paying the mortgage to save her credit and was homeless at the same time.

February was no longer her favorite month of the year.

Tia huffed and tried to swallow her impatience with a deep breath. She wanted to unleash the full scope of her anger, then drown her sorrows in a bottle of something brown that smelled like her grandfather's bedroom.

But the wind whistling through her checkbook would only allow for a half-drunk drowning. That left her with too many un-drunk nerve endings.

She huffed again and enunciated her words. "Will I . . . have to . . . pay Dante?"

Leroy looked unsure. "I don't know."

"Thank you," she said, although, again, it was not what she wanted to hear.

When her father had called from Las Vegas, Nevada, this morning, with his sage advice of deny, deny, deny—he hadn't trusted a cop since 1972—she should have guessed the day wouldn't go well.

But her mother had tricked her and called from a blocked caller ID number, and Tia had stupidly picked up the phone.

"Hello" from Tia had triggered Millicent Amberson, with her five-generation Baptist roots, to start praying. Tia had hung on for the first four minutes, a comb jabbed into her hair, hot curlers smoking on the bathroom sink, and one eye on the clock.

But when her mother asked for forgiveness for trying to raise her child in the way that she should go and failing—"Look at Tia," she'd actually said those words—Tia set down the phone; finished curling her hair; pulled on her stockings, skirt, and jacket; and packed her briefcase.

She picked up the receiver in time to share an amen, then, so as not to seem blasphemous, thought a prayer as she drove in to work with stale raisin toast, between her teeth.

Clearly, her misfortunes were in direct response to her lack of faithful participation.

"Your mom still going to that Holy Roller church?" Leroy asked, looking for middle ground.

Tia sighed. "She and Daddy moved to Vegas, but she's still a card-carrying member."

"It beats the opposite," he said dryly. Five years

ago Leroy's mother, Aunt Julia, had packed up and moved to a colony of self-prescribed witches.

The ground leveled.

"Auntie Millicent still calls and leaves prayers on my answering machine," he added. Guilt tinged Leroy's eyes. "I don't really mind, except she talks up my whole tape."

The earth shifted, and a fissure opened beneath Tia's feet. "She's been known to do that to strangers, too."

"Wow," he said.

"Yep."

Tia let the discomfort sift away with the sieve of distance. She focused on the growing crowd that had gathered outside the courtroom door. She had expected to see well-dressed, clean-cut, remorseful people who were ready to admit to their crime and accept their punishment.

But one group defied the typecasting because of the smiles on their faces. "Who are they?" she asked Leroy.

"All those people have cases to be heard."

Leroy was referring to the fifty or so blacks and Mexicans, a few whites, and one Asian man.

"Now answer my question." Tia glared him.

"They're spectators," he mumbled.

"What?" The hellfire chorus started rehearsing in her stomach. "Is this the new cheap entertainment?"

"There're a few law school students." They both saw one man with a backpack and dreadlocks.

In a quick motion, Tia had Leroy's wrist, her nails poised above a vein.

"Okay." Leroy did the foot-shifting, eye-wandering thing, then shrugged. "Friday court is the substitute

Kings of Comedy." He dared to crack a smile. "Sometimes, it's just funny. I guess word got around."

Luck wasn't something Tia had ever counted on, but she occasionally felt she deserved it. Obviously, the T-shirt she won at fifteen was the extent of it. She massaged her aching forehead. "I can't believe this. I didn't do anything wrong."

"You need to stop saying that. You were cold busted by a cop."

"It's nearly four. I thought the proceedings would be completed by now."

"So you miss the five o'clock news." That was another of her passions, and possibly the reason she and Dante were a couple no more. "What's your rush?"

"I don't belong here," she said loudly. "You think you're better than us" glares were cast her way.

Leroy made her face the wall. "Would you calm down? Everything's under control."

The officers stepped from the courtroom, and everyone gravitated into crooked rows.

Leroy swung them into line, mindful of her healing foot.

"They ought to be ashamed of themselves. People deserve privacy," Tia mumbled, fighting anger.

"Shh."

She ignored him. "They won't get a show from me. You can take the death grip off me now."

"Not until you promise to keep that trigger-happy temper under wraps."

Leroy gave Tia's purse to the officer while she was wanded and searched by another officer.

Humiliated, she stepped on the cold floor while they looked in her shoes.

Why didn't the happy ladies have to take off their shoes?

Leroy must have caught the gist of her thoughts, because he quickly stepped out of his tie-ups, forcing the officer to glance in them.

Tia entered the courtroom. Twelve officers were posted along the walls and in front of the bench.

The spectators chattered away. Everyone else was silent.

What would the judge say to her?

Would he question her motives?

She hoped not, because she still didn't understand why a relationship she'd been willing to commit her life to had ended in such a bizarre manner. She couldn't understand why the man she'd thought herself in love with had done her so wrong. And she couldn't understand why she was being punished and he wasn't.

With the bench empty, the TV screens blank, officers immobile, and the seats filled, she thought of a hundred places she'd rather be.

Helpless anger prompted the hellfire choir in her stomach to hum.

Tia took a seat in the second row, next to Leroy. "Plead me guilty, and get me out of here."

"Tia, these were extenuating circumstances, and the judge will see that. Do you see your arresting officer?"

A tingle ran up her legs to her chest. She didn't want to look. Finding him would, in a sense, confirm her guilt, but she braved her fear and glanced around. Relief and a glimmer of hope moved in her chest. "No. Is that good?"

"Could be. The ADA could ask for a postponement

but will probably drop the charges. The court's calendar is overbooked."

"Why didn't you tell me that before?" she whispered. "I've been worried out of my mind—"

"The ADA told me he's never late for anything. So although he's not here yet, he'll probably show up."

And emotionally, she'd be back where she'd started.

"Don't worry," was all Leroy managed before the judge entered.

"All rise."

Tia said a quick prayer, stood up, and didn't turn around again. If Officer Rivers was there, she'd know soon enough.

Chapter Seven

"Ms. Amberson, you are hereby ordered to take sixty hours of anger management classes."

"Yes, sir," Tia responded to Judge Dunn.

"You're fined two hundred dollars for vandalism."

She whispered to Leroy, and he addressed the court. "Your Honor, the defendant owned the tires."

The judge read the document again. "That may be true, but just as you own your house, you don't have the right to burn it down."

Snickers resounded from the gallery. Give them some popcorn, and they'd be at Magic Johnson's theatre. Judge Dunn looked over his glasses at her, a mischievous grin on his face, and Tia immediately knew two things. The judge was gay. And, when he took off that robe, he was a flaming drama queen.

"Did you say something?" Judge Dunn asked innocently, inviting her to cut up.

"No."

"Did you want to say something?"

Tia licked her teeth and shook her head. No way was she going into her invisible closet and coming out in a sequined dress, five-inch fingernails, and sista girl wig on. "No, sir."

"Ah, well." The judge gave a disappointed sigh. "Is the arresting officer present?"

The assistant district attorney perused the court-room and threw up her hands. "Officer Rivers was supposed to be here."

"I guess this is your lucky day," the judge said to Tia. "The other charges are dropped."

"Uh, Your Honor?" Dante rose from the last row, pulling at the suit Tia had bought him two Christ-mases ago.

Tia's heart hammered. This was the first she'd seen him in weeks.

All the books she'd read on healing from a broken relationship covered this moment. But she didn't feel longing or confusion or loss. She felt pure, uninhibited anger. He'd used her and had been scamming her from the beginning. And now he was here to take the only thing left: her sanity.

He may have played her for a fool, but in the long run, she would win. Knowing this didn't stop the anger.

"May I address the court?" Dante said.

Gleefully, the judge lowered the gavel. "I don't know. Who are you, and what do you want?"

Dante came forward and moved next to the ADA. What did he think he was doing, auditioning for *Law & Order*? "Uh, I'm Dante Manuel, the victim."

This brought giggles from the gallery.

An inch shy of six feet, Dante hardly looked like a victim. More like a down-on-his-luck door-to-door salesman.

Were those extensions in his greasy head? *Yuck.*

Tia made herself look away. With each passing second, the desire to punch him increased. As a precaution, she took two steps closer to the police officer. That way he could easily zap her ankle with his Taser, and she'd avoid a homicide charge.

"Your Honor, it was my car Ms. Amberson vandalized. And I feel that some kind of rectification needs to take place."

Ill-concealed laughter rocked the stuffy courtroom. *Not the big words.* He must have found her *Expand Your Vocabulary* book, looking for the fifty-dollar bill she kept hidden in there for emergencies.

Tia took a deep breath, held it, and started counting. If she calculated correctly, at about 450 seconds, she should drop dead.

"And what type of rectification would you like?" the judge asked, his mental TiVo recording for on-demand playback.

Dante swayed, getting into it. "I think some community service is good, and jail time wouldn't hurt. Uh, I mean, I don't know if she's going to snap again. I mean, she looks fine now, but you never know."

The judge's clerk covered her face with her hands and shook her blond head.

"Mr. Manuel," the judge said, trying to keep a straight face. "You'll have to provide your own personal security if you're scared of Ms. Amberson."

"I didn't say I was scared." Dante looked at Tia—and blinked first. "M-maybe I'll think about that."

"Good." The judge lifted the gavel.

"Uh," Dante interrupted. "Do I get the two hundred dollars the court is collecting?"

Howling, stomping feet, and clapping echoed off

the four walls. The judge bellowed and only stopped laughing to wipe his eyes.

Leroy looked at Tia, and for one moment, they were caught together in the vortex of shame. He objected, to no avail.

Dante had done something she'd never thought would happen to her. He'd bubble-gummed their names under the circus heading freak show.

"She's probably as stupid as him," a woman said, loud enough for Tia to hear. Leroy objected, while the judge tried to restore order.

Tia made a silent vow that if she ever committed another crime of passion, she'd do it in Winder, Georgia, where the probability of the gallery being filled with frightened white people was very high.

The judge's professional face struggled to return. "Mr. Manuel, we don't offer rebates. Ms. Amberson, are there articles that have to be removed from the residence?"

"Sir, the condo is mine. I bought it from the bank after it was foreclosed on. Although it was Mr. Manuel's property *before* and *during* the foreclosure. We were going to live there together, but he made another choice, and consequently, we're not together."

"I see. Well, that changes things."

Tia held her breath.

"I don't think she deserves the place, Your Honor," Dante said. "She bought it for me. That's why *she* left."

The lie slipped easily from Dante's mouth, and for the first time ever, Tia found him to be a believable actor.

The whole relationship had been a lie, and she'd been his sexual and financial means to food, clothing, and shelter. And he'd been her unsuccessful foray into opposites attracting. Where was the love she'd had for him?

Drowned in crab killer and Jheri–curl juice, no doubt.

"Your Honor," Dante continued, "she promised to take care of me in the downtime. Can I get palimony?"

"No!" Judge Dunn bellowed, trying not to lose the battle to another bout of hysterics.

"Shut up," Tia muttered through bared teeth.

"What?" both Dante and Judge Dunn replied.

"Nothing, Your Honor," Leroy said and gave Tia a stern look.

Tia bit her tongue and sniffed the air, smelling smoke. She searched for the source and realized it was her ridiculous life!

She'd dedicated her career to becoming the kind of person people would take seriously. But they wouldn't now. Not after this. If Dante said one more thing . . .

"Ms. Amberson, if there's another outburst, you will be in contempt of court. And the fine is hefty. Fifty dollars a word. Understand?"

Tia didn't move. She felt that if she nodded or spoke, she'd go airborne, leaving the amused cop at her side zapping wind.

"She understands," Leroy answered, a death grip on her elbow. "When can my client regain possession of the property?"

"Seventy-two hours. Officer Rivers can escort her to the property to make sure there are no complications. And that should be enough time for Mr. Manuel to find other accommodations."

Tia wrenched her elbow free. She was fine. As long as Dante didn't say anything else stupid.

"I need more time, Your Honor," Dante said, sounding pitiful.

"Do you work?"

"I'm between projects," he confessed.

The judge sighed dramatically. "And why is that?"

"Because the parts I play are complexual. That's complex and intellectual at the same time. I won't take just anything. The part has to fit me."

"Interesting," the judge said, his hands white against the black robe. "When was the last time you had a role that met your criteria?"

"Two years ago. I had a callback for a movie with Jamie Foxx, but I didn't get it, because of her."

"What did Ms. Amberson do?"

"Your Honor, I don't see how any of this matters," Tia interrupted. "He's in the condo I own."

"Ms. Amberson, please refrain from commenting until called upon. I've already warned you," the judge admonished.

Dante's smug look made her want to scratch his eyes out.

"As I was saying," Dante continued, "I feel that after all the hard work and energy I put into my home, I shouldn't have to give it up to a woman who was just using me for my elite address, among other untangible things."

Tia swayed, while fire from her stomach reached her throat. "Shut up using the wrong words," she said.

The judge banged his gavel. "Quiet," he warned everyone in the courtroom.

"And she gave me a disease," Dante complained loudly.

"You lying dog," Tia exclaimed.

The judge banged the gavel until he was red in the face.

Tia felt her neck being held tightly and realized it was Leroy. "You're going to jail if you say another word, and I'm not going with you! Say something else," he threatened, "and I swear, I'll walk out like I don't know you."

Tia elbowed her cousin away. He wasn't helping her in the least.

"Ms. Amberson," the judge said, "I won't tolerate outbursts in my courtroom."

"What about the fact that he's lying?" Tia demanded. "I see that it's amusing to you and the rest of the people in this courtroom, but it's not a damned bit funny."

"Don't curse," Judge Dunn ordered.

"Excuse me, but he's lying, and you're not stopping him," cried Tia. "Am I supposed to just take it?"

"Yes! I can see that there were no boundaries in this relationship. Since you took matters into your own hands, Ms. Amberson, take responsibility for this. You will be fined fifty dollars for every word hereafter. Mr. Manuel, you have seventy-two hours to vacate the premises, or you'll be held in contempt."

How dare the judge pass judgment on her life? "There were boundaries, Your Honor," Tia said with earnest, "But they didn't include sleeping with other women."

The audience erupted again.

The judge held up his hands, nodding. "Ms. Amberson, I'm warning you for the last time."

Dante's chest had deflated now that the audience was turning on him. "Maybe if you weren't so square, you wouldn't be manless," Dante said, cocky now that she'd been reprimanded. "A little diversity never hurt nobody."

Tia pushed Leroy aside and leaned across the aisle, while Dante hid behind the ADA.

"You non-fucking piece of crap. There aren't two women alive who'd want your scabby little wiener. Go to hell."

"Remove him from my courtroom!" The judge had turned a burnished shade of red and was now standing. Control was gone on both sides of the bench. And Tia didn't care. The judge had allowed a mockery to be made of her life.

"How much is that, Cindy?" the judge bellowed.

"One thousand dollars."

"You have anything else to say, Ms. Amberson?" asked the judge.

"It's the best thousand dollars I've ever spent," Tia retorted, defiant and satisfied for the first time since this debacle began.

Thunderous applause rippled through the room. The judge's gavel clattered onto the desk.

"Deputy, escort Ms. Amberson to the clerk and then out of the building via an exit other than Mr. Manuel's. Ms. Amberson, I feel as if we'll see each other again."

"Not if I can help it."

"Believe me, I hope not too. Dismissed."

Judge Dunn banged the gavel, and Tia turned around.

Officer Byron Rivers stood at the back of the courtroom, an indescribable look on his face. Tia wasn't sure if it was repulsion or embarrassment. Either way, she didn't want to see her life further decimated. He could speak up, and the nightmare would continue.

He was by the book, she'd been told. Never late for anything. A stickler for the law.

Finally, he moved as if in a dream, tipped his head, and was gone.

Tia allowed herself to be led out, hoping she'd never see Dante or the judge again.

If only she could say the same for her arresting officer.

Chapter Eight

"Tia, come into my office, now."

Tia rose from her cube and felt both acute embarrassment and sympathy from her peers. Chance, her boss, had made the demand over the office paging system. Her voice had blared into everyone's work area, which was exactly what she'd intended.

She liked her employees shaking and defenseless before she killed them.

While Tia didn't want to keep Chance waiting, she didn't want to appear afraid, either. She wasn't Chance's bitch, so she took the long way to her office, passing one extra cube before entering the vacuous space.

The distance between the door and Chance's desk seemed to be the length of the Hollywood red carpet, and Chance enjoyed every quaking step her staff had to take before they arrived, intimidated and often crying.

Chance was a size 2 bully.

Tia arrived at the desk, folded her hands, and forced herself not to shake.

"Yes, Chance?"

Pale hands extended from under jet-black sleeves and flipped open Tia's personnel folder.

"Do you know how many days you've been absent this year?"

"Three."

"Six. I'm counting the half days as absences, too. In addition, you've embarrassed this station with your—"

"Chance, I had pneumonia two days in January. Besides, I've already apologized for everything else."

"Else? No, *antics* is a better word. Taken to court by all the local news stations. You were so hideously funny, the AP picked it up. 'I'm sorry' isn't good enough, Tia. We are an organization of professionals, not two-bit hoodlums," she said imperiously. The folder snapped closed. "And you weren't even good at that."

"Chance, I'd had a terrible shock. I'm sorry for causing you or the station any embarrassment. It won't happen again—"

"Excuse me," Chance interrupted sharply. "I'm extending your action plan because of your unprofessional behavior, attendance and poor work performance. If you miss work one day, if you're twelve seconds late, or if you miss one of those anger management classes, I'll take great pleasure in firing you."

"Chance, this is so unnecessary. I had a simple lapse in judgment. It was immature, I know. But believe me, people will forget this with the next big news story."

Chance folded her hands over her waifish stomach. "Now you're an expert? Shouldn't you have thought of that before the profanity flew out of your mouth? Didn't you see the cameras in the courtroom? My God," she exclaimed. "That's why you're not a forecaster now, Tia. You don't use mature discretion. Do you know anything about my personal life? No. Do you see me or anyone else from this office on our rival station as Atlanta's funniest person of the week? No, only you hold that distinguishable honor."

What could she say? Some of what Chance had said was true, but an action plan? She'd been a stellar employee for five years. She'd never used a sick day before this year and had never given her parents, the Normans, a reason to doubt her integrity or commitment to the station. It wasn't until Chance had joined the family business two months ago that Tia had become a problem.

Chance pointed at her, and Tia noticed red marks lining her wrists. When she saw the direction of Tia's gaze, she slapped her hands on the desk. "You have an additional thirty days to convince me not to send you packing. Once my decision is final, my parents won't save you again."

"Please assure them that they won't be disappointed."

"You work for me," she said softly. "Your job is to please me."

The glint in Chance's black-rimmed eyes sent chills up Tia's spine. Her tongue rolled in her mouth as she tried to formulate words that involved mature discretion. "Thank you for the opportunity." *To kick your ass*, her brain completed, but thankfully, the words stayed inside.

"Why are you still standing there? Get back to work."

Tia hadn't wanted to hurry out of Chance's office, but she felt as if Chance's eyes were boring a hole into the back of her head. Before she knew it, she was on the other side, with her back pressed into the handles of the door.

Ronnie/Rhonda, the cross-dressing mail clerk, sashayed up, dressed as a woman today. "I'd have kicked my sister's bitch ass. You held your ground, though. Good for you."

Tia sprinted after him. He was six feet four and had a stride like a gazelle. "How do you know what went on in there?"

"Baby, Rhonda knows everything. Now get to your desk before you're on the street. She's coming."

Her heartbeat thundered as Tia careened up the side aisle of workstations and duckwalked to her seat. She landed just in time.

"I thought you were going to make my job easy," Chance said from behind her, making the hairs on Tia's neck stand up. "Sign these."

Tia squeezed her hands before turning around and taking the papers. The other meteorologists and various assistants were all huddled in their cubes like frightened kittens.

The papers outlined her action plan and the performance review she hadn't seen. She leafed through it and saw the low scores. "I'd like the opportunity to read this over. On my own time, of course. May I return this to personnel tomorrow?"

Tia knew she was pushing her luck, but Chance couldn't skirt the law, no matter how much she hated her.

"Nine a.m. sharp. Sign the other one now."

Furious, Tia scribbled her name and thrust the action plan back at Chance, who grinned. "Ah, so the peacock awakens." She snatched the papers. "Get to work."

Tia turned to her desk and looked at the reports she needed to complete. The worst part of her job was that sometimes it was just plain boring. Her assignment for the past month had been to review data from Alaskan meteorologists, who, on a daily basis, measured glacial melting. Not exactly her dream job, but someone had to do it.

She tried not to think about it as she plugged in figures for the next three hours.

She typed in numbers that resembled her bank PIN and realized she needed to check her account balance. Craning her neck to see if Chance was around, Tia typed in her banking institution and accessed her account. $897.04. That was all the money in her checking account. She already knew her savings account was empty.

Her heart rate increased by ten beats a minute as she memorized the withdrawals, closed the screen, and returned to the weather Web sites before getting her checkbook out of her purse.

The card for the anger management class fell out. *Damn.* She still had to face that awful music.

"Want to do lunch with us?" Ronnie/Rhonda asked.

Tia fumbled with the checkbook. "You need to make some noise and stop sneaking around, scaring people."

"The guilty always protest too much," Ronnie/

Rhonda said, with a sweet grin, his eyes bright blue. "Hungry, peacock?"

Tia glanced at the card, knowing somehow that the class wasn't going to be either free or cheap. "I'd better not, but thanks."

"Don't let that Morticia freak get to you." Ronnie/Rhonda's voice rose a bit.

"I'm not," Tia said to quiet him. "I've got something to do, that's all."

Tia didn't fold under the intense scrutiny. The last thing she needed was to cause a scene. That would surely get her fired. And she'd make Chance's day.

"All righty then. Come on, girls," Ronnie/Rhonda said to the two station interns who stood dutifully behind him. "We're lunching on the outdoor patio at Blanco's so we can babe watch an hour of our life away. Ciao."

"Ciao," Tia said, as the group weaved to the elevator and left her in miserable silence. She and Ronnie/Rhonda had never been close friends, but the cross-dressing man was always good for a laugh and gossip every now and then.

Not for the first time, Tia wondered why he'd been kept on at the station. Two years ago, he'd started as a man and then one day showed up as a woman. The staff had been aflutter and his parents hadn't been happy, but Ronnie/Rhonda had endeared himself to the people at WKTT and now he was a treasured member of the staff. The truth was, he knew something about everything and that made him invaluable.

Tia eyed her checkbook again. The state had cashed her thousand-dollar check in a hurry.

She dialed the number on the card for the class

and waited. Instructions were given, and then her mouth fell open. She pressed ONE to hear the message again. "Registration for the anger management class is $295. If you are registered before five p.m. eastern standard time tomorrow you will be enrolled in the class that begins tomorrow night at 7:30 p.m. at Reynolds High School. To register using a credit card only, please press two."

Tia disconnected the call, then redialed. Her fingers hovered over the 2. That was three hundred dollars. She needed that money for other important stuff.

Like that cute Kate Spade purse she'd eyed on eBay.

The judge's words haunted her, as did Chance's.

She didn't have a choice.

Tia pressed TWO and entered her credit card number, then ran to the bathroom stall for a good cry. *This better be worth it,* she vowed as she hunkered over the toilet, relieving herself.

The outer door opened and closed.

"Of course I was serious about your niece working here," Chance said into her cell phone. "I just have to clear up a personnel issue, and then we're all set. Two weeks, tops."

Tia had stopped peeing midstream. She cringed at her only option and let her bare ass hit the seat. Quietly, she put her feet on the door and prayed she didn't catch anything else communicable.

"The job will be vacant in two weeks. The idiot in it won't last. Right, of course. I didn't mean to offend you. Good-bye, Miss . . ." Chance's voice trailed off as she snapped her phone closed. "What was I thinking? Why did I say that? God, I'm in trouble. I've got to get Tia out of here, or I'm toast."

Tia strained as her butt started to slip on the seat.

The outer door opened and closed with a hiss, and Chance was gone.

Tia let her legs down and shot off the seat. She vowed to soak off the germs tonight, righted her clothes, and left the stall. Washing her hands, she was back at her desk in under a minute.

She was the idiot Chance had been speaking of. Why had her job already been promised to someone else?

Well, she wasn't going to make it easy for Chance to fire her. In fact, she was going to be employee of the freaking year if it killed her.

Chapter Nine

The corner of Tenth and Piedmont wasn't a normal hookers' hangout, but construction on Luckie Street had driven business in.

The calls about the trash and activity had started coming in at midnight, an hour into Byron's shift. He'd responded with increased patrols, sometimes flashing his lights, but as soon as he pulled away, they'd resurface, like cockroaches, and claim the corners again.

Unsettled, he drove the streets, wishing everyone would just go home and go to sleep. That's where he wanted to be. At home. Asleep.

Alone. There wasn't another option, considering he didn't have anyone.

That was cool, he reminded himself. His last girl-friend, Lynn, had driven him crazy with her suspicious, jealous ways.

But could cook. And she could make him lose his mind in bed. More than once he'd been glad for the half acre of space between his house and his neighbors. Or else he'd have had some explaining to do.

He directed his patrol car up Fourteenth and down Piedmont Avenue, heading back toward the heart of the city.

He and Lynn were over. For good. And no amount of reminiscing would change that. She was crazy. A drama queen with no throne.

Months ago he'd made himself delete her number from his cell phone, but he still remembered it.

His cell phone rang, surprising him.

Lynn.

Had he talked her up, or what?

He hesitated over whether to answer, then pushed the phone icon. "Byron Rivers."

"You sound just as sexy as ever. Hello, handsome."

Damn.

She sounded like rain after a long drought. Her voice made him want to vacation in its sweetness for a hot minute. But this was Lynn. His ex for a reason. "What's up, Lynn?"

"Missing you. You been thinking about me?"

"Not really," he lied.

"You weren't ever a good liar. That's why I was always glad to use you as an expert witness. Juries believe you. I've been thinking about us."

"At two in the morning?" he asked. "Ten months after you walked out? Why would I be crossing your mind?"

"You were the best thing that ever happened to me, and I blew it. I know I did. But the best part about making a mistake is forgiveness. You told me that once."

Her sexy voice lured him but didn't make him

forget. "You left me. I wasn't ambitious enough, re-member? I'm still the same beat cop who only makes enough money to eat out once a week."

He drove to the edge of his territory, then headed back in.

"Now who's holding a grudge? I'm a changed woman. You'll see. What time do you get off?"

"You know." She was an attorney and had connec-tions everywhere. "Just like you knew I was working."

Her husky laugh took him back to some of their better days.

"Can I make your breakfast?"

"I don't—"

"A man has to eat. Bacon, waffles, grits, eggs," she purred. "Coffee with cream. I haven't lost my touch. You'll be completely satisfied."

The offer hung out there like a seller hawking tickets. Maybe he was being too close-minded. "All right. Breakfast and that's it."

She laughed again. "See you at eight a.m. at your place. Be safe."

As soon as the call disconnected, second thoughts ran through his mind. Lynn Summer, a defense at-torney from Chicago, had a plan for her life that included a man who wasn't Byron. He didn't make six figures or more, nor did he see himself getting close to that in the foreseeable future.

Lynn, who loved the finer things in life, was the same woman who'd left with every designer bauble he'd ever bought her.

Except his broken heart. She hadn't placed much value on that. He tried to dial her back but didn't get even her voice mail. She was trouble. Just like Tia Amberson.

Byron slapped his forehead and stomped on the brakes. He had to register for the anger management class. He dug out the number, dialed, and paid, pissed.

Women were nothing but trouble.

He cruised past a parking lot, saw the same action, and stopped.

He amended his earlier thoughts about women. *People* were crazy.

He called in the public sex act and got out of his patrol car. The couple was too engaged to notice him.

He tapped the kneeling woman on the shoulder with his billy club. "Police. Stop what you're doing, and get up."

The man reacted first. His eyes shot open. He jerked to the right. Unfortunately, he must have met teeth, because he started squealing and running in place.

The hooker turned around, unfazed. "Cain't you see we're busy?"

"Breaking the law. Get up. You're under arrest."

"Really?" she said.

Damn, Byron thought. This wasn't going to be easy.

Suddenly, dirt sprayed his face. Temporarily blinded, he grabbed hold of the freakishly strong woman. Luckily, she was still kneeling. They wrestled for a minute, with Byron grinding his teeth when her nails dug into his arm. Ten seconds later, he had her subdued, and within a minute, she was in the back of his patrol car.

Outside the car, he went through her bag while she cussed and kicked at the window.

"Hey," Byron hollered at her. "You better not mess up my car."

He just prayed she didn't defecate on the back-seat. That was the worst.

Byron radioed the station. "Run a check on Strawberry Jones. Five-foot-ten female, 185 pounds."

Several seconds passed. "It's a hit," came back the dispatcher. "Wanted in three counties in Georgia, and in Alabama for solicitation. The other charges range from assault with deadly, assault on a police officer, threatening a witness, and jaywalking. She's a badass."

Byron looked at the thrashing hooker and gathered her stuff off the hood. His arms were bleeding, and the threat of impending doom seemed to have come to rest on his shoulders.

The john had gotten away. But, Byron reasoned, hopefully, this bust would help get him off the night shift and get his career back on track. Byron wasn't normally morbid, but somehow he didn't think so.

Chapter Ten

Old memories resurfaced as Byron walked through the white-walled halls of Reynolds High School, his alma mater. Although the school had been remodeled and upgraded to accommodate twenty-three hundred students, the unpleasant years he'd spent here couldn't be glossed over with new paint.

He'd been a boy of small stature; "underdeveloped," his mother liked to say apologetically to her church lady friends.

His father promised he'd grow up thick and tall one day. For Byron, someday had been too far away. The daily torture of being knocked around Reynold's waxed floors had been frustrating.

He was grown now, yet here he still felt unsettled.

At the end of the hallway, he consulted the paper in his hand.

Anger Management: Room 100.9. He looked up again. 100.7. 100.17. 100.27. Across the hall were 101.7 and 101.17.

He'd just come from 102.7.

What kind of numbering system was this? He tried applying an equation but grew more frustrated. In five minutes, he'd be late for his first anger management class.

Good. He was mad, anyway.

Two girls dressed in cheerleader uniforms approached.

"Ladies, can you direct me to 100.9?"

The tallest girl slid the paper from his hand. "Don't you get the sequence? This hallway is all sevens."

Oh.

"Go down two corridors. Take the steps down. Through the double doors, fifty paces. Turn left, and you'll be on the nines corridor. Ninth door on your left."

He must have looked confused, because the shorter girl yanked a pen from behind her ear and took the paper. "Here, let me show you."

When Byron looked down, he swallowed. She'd drawn a "you are here" map on the back, and an illustrated guide.

"Thanks," he mumbled. To his dismay, they followed him, to make sure he'd made the correct turn, before going on their way.

Two minutes later, he was outside the room. A steady hum of pleasant voices filtered into the hallway, and Byron felt a smidgen of relief. Maybe this wouldn't be so bad, after all.

He stepped into the room, and every mouth shut.

No, this would be worse.

Ten angry women glared at him as if he alone were responsible for labor pains, PMS, and the disproportionate number of men's and women's restrooms at the football stadium.

"Is this anger management?" he asked, hoping against hope it wasn't.

"Yes." The instructor, a short man with even shorter sleeves, stood behind the desk, his credibility decimated by the length of his comb-over. The look of fear in his eyes didn't help, either.

"I thought this class was for men only."

Angry murmurs resounded from the natives. "No," the man responded, letting Byron hang in idiotic limbo alone.

"Great," Byron said.

Byron heard his response in his head and ventured to see the reaction. They were pissed. He hadn't meant to offend them. Nevertheless, he wished he had his Kevlar vest, gun, pepper spray, cuffs, and billy club.

These women didn't appear to need provocation to devour him and then pick their teeth with his bones.

Maybe if he sat down, they'd forget he was there.

Byron headed up the aisle and was confronted by their size 4X leader. Frustration prickled that he wasn't in his uniform. Had he been, he'd have ordered her back. However, his student status didn't allow for a coup de grace. So he retreated and twisted his ankle on a well-placed booby trap—a purse.

Evil snickers filled the room.

Because the air was charged with X chromosome energy, he feared if he didn't diffuse the women, he'd disappear from society and emerge years later, wearing an apron and, he swallowed, pearls.

He tried to squeeze by their leader, who had her forehead to his chest, but her stout legs held firmly at a ninety-degree angle—enough to turn her into a steel girder.

Every time she inhaled, his legs slipped a little, until his hamstrings were pressed solidly against the unrelenting table behind him.

To gain the advantage, he exhaled and caved his chest.

Another tactical error, Byron realized when the sumo's body filled the space. Oxygen whooshed from his mouth. His lungs panicked and screamed for air.

The woman received encouragement from her friends. "Go on, girl!"

"He ain't nothin' but rude!"

"Show him who's boss!"

His brain received an instant message from his lungs: breathe now or die. "If you'd just let—" he said and stopped. He was going to pass out.

Just before the silver stars in his eyes turned black, she popped through, and he gulped in air.

"No, you didn't just call me fat!"

Byron stared at her in disbelief. She'd almost killed him! "I didn't call you fat."

"I heard you. You called me fat," she told the indignant mob.

"I heard him, too," a woman said, although she was two tables away.

"I never said that!" "I'm a cop," he wanted to declare but didn't. Who'd believe him in a mob of angry women?

The instructor finally interceded. "It's over now. Everyone, please take your seats."

Was that the best he could do? The little wimp wouldn't even look Byron in the eye.

Byron touched the chair the big woman had vacated. A purse landed on the plastic. "Taken."

He moved across the aisle. "Taken."

He touched another. "Taken."

He threw up his hands. "Fine. Which of these seats isn't taken?"

The lady at the fifth table from the front pointed to a chair in the back of the room.

"That's just great." Byron grabbed the seat and planted it firmly against the last table and sat.

He leaned back, and the chair groaned. Forced to hunch forward, Byron couldn't help but remember how little he'd liked school.

The instructor approached him. "You should apologize for calling Pebbles fat."

Pebbles? What sensible grown-up would have the nickname of a cartoon character? A little white tag on the instructor's breast pocket announced his name.

"Look here, Fred. I didn't call her fat, so I'm not apologizing."

Fred sucked up brownie points by showing his disappointed frown to the class.

"Don't you see what's happening? If we don't stick together, we're dog food." Byron tried to establish a sense of brotherhood with the man, but he knew it was a lost cause.

"I'll have to report your lack of cooperation," Fred said loudly.

And that would be all Captain Hanks needed to have his badge. "Wait." Byron hated not having choices. He chewed the inside of his jaw before forcing his lips to move. "I didn't call you fat, but I apologize if you misheard me."

He'd managed to elicit consternation from every person in the room.

"How is that a real apology?" Pebbles demanded.

Even Fred looked confused. "Well, that's a good beginning." He headed to the front of the room. "My name is Fred, and we're here because you're all dealing with a similar issue. Making good use of your anger."

The door flew open and banged against the wall, and Tia Amberson walked in.

Byron wasn't the least bit surprised. If the big rock that was Stone Mountain were to shrink to the size of a marble, he wouldn't have batted an eye.

Surprise was the norm in his life lately.

"Sorry I'm late." Tia hurried in, oblivious to the disruption she caused. "I've been looking for this room for twenty minutes. The numbers aren't sequential."

Dressed in black pants and black-heeled boots, she marched around like she owned the place. She scrawled her name on a blank name tag, growing exasperated when she couldn't peel off the waxy back.

Tearing it in half, she finally peeled it apart, slapped the sticky back on her chest, and ended up in front of Fred, whose mouth hung open. "Here's my paperwork," she said.

Flustered, Fred tried to find the words. "I can't

allow you in this class. Timeliness and perfect attendance are requirements."

She looked at his chest. "Fred, I already explained that I couldn't find the room. So how about you giving me a break?"

"M-m-my hands are tied."

Tia folded her arms over her chest and walked toward the already too close instructor. "Fred, I'm here for anger management because I'm angry! So, unless you're willing to mark me absent, which we know isn't true, I'm staying." With that, she plopped into a chair and crossed her legs.

Fred wiped his comb-over twice, his eyes wide.

"You should let her in," Pebbles told Fred. "You can see she's got issues."

Tia looked at the woman. "Thank you. No wonder kids flunk out of school. They can't ever find their classrooms."

The other women chuckled in agreement.

Byron watched the exchange as if it were a bad play in community theatre.

"Oh, okay. Th-this one . . . just once," Fred finally managed. "Let's get down to business."

Byron wondered how long it would be before Tia saw him.

"Introduce yourself. Starting in the back."

"I'm Roxy," the woman said a table up from Byron.

Tia turned around, saw Byron, and gathered her things. "Is there another class offered at this same time?" she asked Fred.

"No." He backpedaled like a frightened golden retriever.

She shouldered her bag. "I guess I'll have to do my thirty days in jail."

Fred danced like a fire had started in his pocket protector. "I said you could stay, Ms. Uh"—he squinted, a good four inches below the name tag she'd stuck near her shoulder—"wow."

"Like what you see?" Tia snapped her jacket, and Fred jumped. "Can men only read at breast level?"

"I wasn't looking at your bre-b—"

"What's my name?" Tia demanded.

"Uh . . ." Fred looked like he needed a bathroom. "I don't know."

"Case closed. Can we move on?" Tia remained standing.

Byron pitied Fred, who had wiped his comb-over so often, it had crested at the crown of his head. Then he collapsed in his chair.

"Please, somebody introduce yourself. Give a brief explanation as to why you're here. Start here." Fred motioned to Tia, without looking.

"I'm Tia. I'm here because my ex-fiancé cheated on me, and I got caught redecorating his car by a heartless police officer who thought I was making a play for him when I was really fainting, then gave me a black eye, and arrested me, anyway."

The gushed words came to an abrupt halt.

"What a jerk," Roxy said. "He's probably jealous because he doesn't have a woman."

Ouch.

Breakfast with Lynn had been an illusion. Having her at his house when he got home this morning had made him want her there.

Someone there, he corrected. Not necessarily her. Yet, he hadn't told her not to come back tomorrow.

"She'd probably leave him because he's too busy minding other people's business and not earning any money," the purse lady said.

"Get him fired," Pebbles added. "I'll bet most of us are here because of a man."

The women started clapping like they were in church. Byron wondered why Tia didn't out him.

"I'd like to go next," said a soft-spoken woman two rows from the front. "My name is Ginger Kelston—"

"Don't give your last name, please," Fred said.

"Okay." She began again. "I'm Ginger, no last name, and I was sent here by my family therapist, who thinks I have anger issues, because I sleepwalk."

The woman across from Ginger gave her a suspicious look. "You sleepwalk? That's it?"

Ginger laughed, and her russet hair bobbed. "Well, I've been arrested three times for trying to board a plane, bus, and train with semiautomatic weapons in my possession."

"Where were you going, and what were you going to do with them, Ginger?" Fred asked as he eased toward the door.

Punk.

"It seems I'm always heading to Utah, where my husband moved a month ago with all of my inheritance so he could become a polygamist."

The class went absolutely still.

Ginger threw her clueless hands into the air and sat down. "Crazy, huh?"

Nobody spoke for a full minute.

"Why aren't you locked up somewhere?" Pebbles asked.

"Because I'm not on drugs. And I haven't done anything wrong," Ginger responded with an airy laugh.

"N—n—next?" Fred backed into the dry erase board and scared himself.

The big lady rolled to her feet. "Hey," she drawled in her native Georgian tongue. "I'm Pebbles. I destroyed the master bathroom in my home after I learned my husband had another woman in there. See." She showed her hands to Ginger. "No guns. You ever heard of a life sentence? Death penalty mean anything to you?"

"I've never fired a gun in my life," Ginger stated matter-of-factly.

"All right. *The Three Faces of Eve.* Just remember none of us is your cheating man."

"Don't worry, Pebbles. I won't hurt anyone," Ginger said, but her sanguine smile made a few of the women shudder.

The other ladies admitted to various misdemeanors, but Byron stopped keeping track and made a mental note to update the beneficiaries in his will.

He finally stood. "I'm Byron, and I had a disagreement with my boss."

Pebbles glared at him. "Did you hit him?"

"No."

"But you wanted to, right?"

"The thought crossed my mind."

Tia didn't turn all the way around, but Byron knew he had her attention.

"Was he white or black?" Pebbles wanted to know.

"That doesn't matter," screeched Fred, who was white. "Color has no bearing on anger. This class is racially mixed, but you share one common bond. You're here to learn how to control a very complex emotion. Anger is one of the most honest emotions we humans possess. Along with hunger and the desire to have our basic needs met, anger is an alert system to the body when something isn't right.

"We've all seen children have tantrums. They haven't learned reasoning skills, but they can and do get angry. Anger can be raw, powerful, and potentially harmful if a mechanism isn't put into place to control it. You're going to learn techniques to help you deal with your anger."

Fred passed out textbooks and wire-bound notebooks. "For homework, read chapters one through five. Also, for the duration of the class, you'll be required to keep a journal."

A collective groan moved through the group. "I'm not keeping a journal," Debbie said, as she sat across from Ginger. "Anything you write can be used against you in a court of law."

A chorus of dissenters agreed, and notebooks hit the tabletops in protest. "Forget it," was the consensus.

"Ladies, you have to," Fred squealed, failing to talk over them. "Listen to me. I'm the teacher."

Byron dropped his head. This guy was a disgrace to men everywhere.

"It's time for a break." Pebbles put her purse on her arm and waddled toward the door, women trailing her. "We might have to call it an early night if this is all you've got to say."

Fred stood in front of the class, visibly shaking. "I've devised a set of rules, per se, things I've found have helped me when I feel myself getting angry. Anger is a healthy emotion, but it can also be a fool's worst enemy." He grinned, although it came off looking like he'd been kicked in the spleen. "I call them Fred's Rules for Fools."

Nobody in the room moved. Fred's leg shook as if he were a potty-training toddler. He laughed and it sounded like a whimper. "Okay." He spoke in a voice much too high for a man with an Adam's apple. "They're pasted inside the front cover of your journals, but we'll review them weekly. The first rule is, when in a disagreement with a person, stick to the subject and never repeat yourself."

Byron felt sorry for Fred. He was going to get beat up by a bunch of women because he was as lame as his rules. Rules for Fools.

Use "I feel," rather than accuse. Walk away. Acknowledge when you're wrong. Don't make idle threats. Forgive those that have wronged you. Take responsibility for your anger. Don't instigate. Channel your anger by working out/exercising to the point of exhaustion. Focus on breathing techniques—in through nose and out through nose. When you're really concentrating, nothing can make you angry. You are responsible for your emotions. Guard them intensely, and use them wisely.

Pebbles moved like a sumo wrestler to Fred's desk. "How are you ever going to get your point across if you can't reference what happened in the past? Especially if you know he's done something back then that you can use in your argument now."

"Can you ever recall a time when, in an argument, you changed the other person's mind by saying something over and over again?" asked Fred.

"No, but—"

"That's it then." Fred nodded conclusively, as if he'd won the debate team trophy. "Let's move on to class expectations."

"But I wasn't finished," Pebbles said loudly.

"What new item do you want to bring to the discussion, Ms. Pebbles?" He sounded defeated. Emotionally, she was beating his ass with his trophy.

"New? We're still on the old. How is not repeating myself going to stop my husband from bringing other women in my house?"

"I don't know," said Fred.

The class glared at Fred.

"What?" mumbled Roxy, who sat at the table ahead of Byron. "No, I didn't pay good money to hear you say you don't know something. I know I'd better get better answers than that. If you think I'm mad now, see me when you've wasted my time and my hard-earned cash."

"You may have to accept that the infidelity happened and forgive him. Rule number six," Fred told Pebbles. "Otherwise, I-I don't know."

"You repeated yourself," Ginger told him gently.

"I know." Fred looked like he was getting fried on the sidewalk, under a magnifying glass.

"That's okay because it was another person asking the question. So technically, you're not repeating yourself to Ms. Pebbles if you answered someone else." Then Ginger gave the class the smile of an angel.

Byron watched the byplay and wondered if this class was for the mentally ill or if he was just unlucky.

"I promise this works. If you use this technique, you will find disagreements shorter and less painful."

"Not at my house," Pebbles grunted. "We can go at it for hours."

A chorus of agreement supported her. "Fred, I don't think you know what you're talking about."

The dissenters grew louder.

"If you're not going to change that person's mind, why get yourself all worked up?" Fred asked the class.

"Because sometimes, you have to say it again to make yourself feel better." Ginger, the redhead, spoke to the unseen husband who'd taken up with several wives in Utah. "Like you're not talking just to hear yourself speak."

For a scared little man, Fred moved quickly to block the doorway. "You have to write in the journals and copy down today's rule, o-or you can't take a break."

"Do you know what we could do to you?" Pebbles mashed her girth into Fred until he was barely visible above her mammoth breasts. He looked like an eraser.

"I'll tell on you," Fred said, as he slowly turned crimson.

He'd suffocate if she didn't get off of him soon.

"I don't mind writing in mine." Tia scrawled her name inside the front cover of her journal and laid it on the table at her seat.

Byron contained his surprise. He'd expected Tia

to be the first person to line up behind Pebbles. From all he'd seen of her, especially at court, she was a straight hell-raiser. A rebel with a minor cause.

"I know I've got anger issues, especially against the cop that arrested me, my ex, and my boss," Tia said.

Damn. She did have issues, but Tia spoke a truth few wanted to acknowledge. Even him.

Reluctantly, slowly, a few women agreed.

Pebbles considered the words of her fellow women friends. "We'll think about it."

Fred was quick to agree. "I think it's time to take a break."

"Great idea." Pebbles marched through the door.

With his back against the wall, Fred guarded the square below his belt with a three-ring notebook.

"Why are you letting her run all over you?" Byron asked him.

"I'm taking a course on becoming more assertive, and they suggested teaching. I have the credentials, the degrees." Fred sighed and flopped into his chair behind the desk. "I suck, don't I?"

Byron didn't want the man to have a nervous breakdown. He gave Fred's shoulder a whack of encouragement. "You'll get better." *I hope.* "You want something to drink?"

"No, I think I'll put my head down for a few minutes. Women make me tired."

Byron blanched at the confession but left Fred to his rest period. At least the man knew when he was in over his head.

The murmurs of women getting to know one another caught up to Byron, and he entered the

commons area and saw them huddled around two
small tables, flashing wallet photos, lockets, and
mothers' rings.

Women had an uncanny ability of getting to
know one another. They only needed a single
common thread, and the next thing you knew, they
were thanking God for bringing them a lifelong
friend, and next, talking about the fun they had on
a cruise.

He shoved four quarters into the soda machine,
got his soda, popped the lid, and swallowed the
liquid in gulps.

Men were less complex.

Men didn't talk to men they didn't know.

Men didn't vacation together.

And men never, ever flashed pictures.

If they found themselves in a discussion with another man, the topic was always sex and included
the expressions "hittin' it" and "waxin' that ass."

Men were streamlined thinkers, and Byron appreciated that about his compatriots.

The rules shifted if men and women were in the
same room.

Everything a man said from the moment he met
a woman was designed with one purpose in mind:
Was he going to get laid?

Am I going to get laid?

Byron adjusted his waistband but let go. He applied the theory of deductive reasoning and got an
immediate answer.

No woman, no nooky.

Damn.

"I didn't know you had dimples," Tia said.

Caught unaware, Byron sucked a little too hard on the can and scratched the inside of his upper lip. He waited a few seconds for the pain to subside. "It's a well-kept secret."

"You'd appear more friendly if you let it out sometimes."

He ignored the criticism. "You're welcome."

"For what?"

"Court."

She inserted four quarters and pressed the button for her soda. "Thanks. I hope you didn't expect me to fall at your feet." When he didn't respond, Tia chuckled. "You're hilarious."

The laughter stung more than the insult. "It was a gift."

"Then you need to start over in the first grade and learn what a gift really is."

Frustration worked through his nervous system. She was the reason he was here in the first place. "I shouldn't have expected gratitude from you. You fled custody. The judge should have thrown the book at you."

"Who threw the book at you, Byron? What kept you from seeing me behind bars for six months?" Her chocolate brown eyes held him hostage. "You're in trouble because of me, aren't you?"

"No."

Her smile said she didn't believe him. "You'd have testified against me if you'd made it in time. But you're here. Coincidence? I don't think so. We aren't so different."

He harrumphed his disagreement.

"I wasn't angry until that night changed my life.

Now I can't seem to shake it. So that means I have to go wherever it takes me. We're here for similar reasons. I'm almost sure of that." She assessed him through eyes that smiled for her. "This class just got interesting."

"If you have any ideas of retaliation against your ex, I'll get you, and I'll make it stick."

Challenge sparkled in her eyes. "I'll keep checking my tail to see if you're on to me. See you around, Officer."

Tia headed back to the tables and hunched down in the circle of women.

When they all turned to look at him, he left the commons area and prayed he hadn't just activated the female version of an atomic bomb.

Chapter Eleven

Tia slid into her chair at work with two minutes to spare, angry that she hadn't awakened earlier, as she'd planned.

"Cutting it close, aren't you?"

Chance's voice hissed against her neck, and Tia forced herself not to react. That was how Chance got her kicks.

"I'm here. On time. That's all that matters."

"That mouth is going to be your downfall."

Tia used a technique she'd learned while reading her homework chapter and didn't respond.

"Nothing to say?"

"If you'll excuse me, I've got to prepare for the broadcast."

Chance's smile bloomed. "Reassignment. Alison is sitting in as backup anchor for Ben."

The ever-present simmer in Tia's stomach began to boil. "What? Why?"

"We need an experienced, mature person in line, should anything happen to Ben."

"She's an intern! Alison can't even pronounce

cumulus. She says cunnilingus. How inappropriate is that? Doesn't that concern you?"

"What an exaggerator you are." Chance laughed, looking cool and pasty. "But at this point, you'd say anything to get your butt out of trouble. As for Alison, this is Georgia. If she ever gets on the air, it's highly unlikely she'll ever have to use the word. You're reassigned. You're proofreading copy for the Web site."

That's what Alison does, Tia wanted to say but didn't.

Interns did the grunt work. That was a universal rule of life. But this was Chance's opportunity to try to force her to quit so her friend's niece could take her job. Tia hated it, but her twelve-hundred-dollar mortgage kept her from ripping Chance's head off, thus saving the evil woman's life.

"Fine. I'll read copy."

"Very good." Chance clapped her milky hands, looking annoyed and frustrated.

Tia put on her best innocent face. "You should get something for that rash."

"I beg your pardon?"

"Your wrists," she whispered loudly. "Hydrocortisone cream should knock it right out. Unless it's fungal."

Chance looked as if she'd gulped down a bucket of razors. "Don't concern yourself with me."

"I wasn't."

"Sister, you're two shakes away from being on the outside, looking in at all of us employed people."

"Don't threaten me." Tia's control slipped. Heat

grew under her butt, and she inched to the end of her chair.

"I don't threaten. That's a promise."

Chance stomped away in impossibly high-heeled boots. She suffered from the female version of the Napoleon syndrome. She thought she was a dictator, when she was just a mini Fred Flintstone.

Tia rushed to the bathroom, stinging from the informal demotion. What would everyone think? She'd come to WKTR Television six months before Ben. And while he'd been promoted several times and was now the on-air anchor, she'd been shoved into research and now proofreading.

Tia stared at her face in the mirror and tried to think pleasant thoughts.

Less than a minute in, she gave up. What a load of crap. She was getting screwed! How could Chance have chosen Alison? The girl was a nymphomaniac.

Well, there was always a chance that Chuck would get food poisoning and Alison would commit a sex act on the air.

A little giggle bubbled up from her chest, and Tia finally felt some relief. Maybe she should fight anger with laughter.

She'd have to ask Fred to talk about it in class, the little runt.

Another laugh bubbled up, and Tia threw the damp paper towels she'd put on her neck in the trash and headed back to her desk.

She'd found a new way to fight her fiery emotions. She'd laugh the rest of her life away.

***

By three o'clock, Tia thought she'd strangle the next person who stopped by to check on her. Laughing had given her a headache and had caused more than one person to offer to pray for her.

Ronnie/Rhonda drove up as Ronnie today. "Hey, sista girl. I hear you're pulling a Jack Nicholson on everybody with all that laughing."

Tia didn't feel like being bothered, but Ronnie had always been nice to her. She sighed. "What?"

"*One Flew Over the Cuckoo's Nest,*" he said and laughed. "You'd have been better off saying, 'Hello, Clarice.'" He did a perfect imitation of Anthony Hopkins. "At least then they'd know what the hell they're dealing with."

Tia rested her hand under her chin and grinned. "You're crazy. You know that?"

"Yep, and that's why these devils leave me alone. I'll go straight nutso/whacko on their asses, and this whole place would get turned upside down. Welp, I'd better tootle. The dragon just left her den. Here." He handed her a white bag.

"What's this?" she whispered.

"I like my women with a little ass, and you, my dear, won't have one if you don't eat. Ciao."

Tia's eyes widened, and she couldn't move. Ronnie/Rhonda was a real dude inside?

Tia stopped her careening thoughts. Nine out of ten days Ronnie/Rhonda was a girl. If there was a man in that body, he sure wouldn't be tricked out in red ruffles every Monday, with his hair pinned up.

Unless he was Prince.

There were exceptions to every rule.

"Thank you," she stage-whispered outside of her cube.

"Da nada, baby," Ronnie said, before gliding into the elevator with his mail cart.

Tia wasn't sure how he'd heard her, but that didn't matter. He'd done a good deed and fed the hungry.

She opened the turkey and lettuce wrap and thanked God for Ronnie/Rhonda's sweet soul. It was Atkins friendly.

Tia closed her burning eyes, savoring her unexpected lunch. Ronnie/Rhonda didn't know that he'd saved her from a humiliation worse than dying in your ex's chimney.

She had thirty dollars in the bank until payday, and that was three days away. Buying dinner wasn't an option. She racked her brain for food possibilities.

Happy hour.

Tia warmed inside.

She bit into the last piece of her wrap, logged onto the Internet and accessed a map of downtown Atlanta. There were thirty hotels between here and the interstate. She checked off the ones that had three stars or lower, had suites in the title, and were more than a fifteen-minute drive away.

Ten remained. She printed the list, then hurried to get it, glancing over her shoulder every step of the way. She chided herself for being careless.

If she weren't on an action plan, making a personal copy wouldn't have been a problem, but now her every move was under the microscope.

Back in her cube, Tia was reviewing the list when her phone buzzed. She could see from the caller ID that it was Rachel. She worked her jaw before answering.

"Hello?"

"Hey. Didn't see you this morning."

"That's because you and Kyle were . . . involved."

"We're in love, Tia. I'd hoped you could understand that."

"What is it, Rachel? I've got to get going."

"I just got a disturbing call from Sonny."

"What did he want?"

"Apparently Megan's been stalking him."

"Why would you believe that?"

"Because she traded in her car and took a leave of absence from work. She was at the airport today, when he and his wife got home from their honeymoon."

"There could be a perfectly good reason for her being at the airport. It is the largest airport in the world."

"Lot C, section B. That's where he was parked. She was in lot C, section C, sitting there, he said, crying."

"That's a little spooky, but before I take his word for anything, I'd like to hear from Megan."

"Good. I thought we could perform an intervention tonight at her house."

Megan wasn't known for having food. "Uh, why not at the Hilton at six-thirty? That way nobody can cause a scene and tell somebody to get out."

"True," Rachel agreed.

"I'm kind of short on cash, so I can't treat."

"Don't worry. It's on me."

Tia regretted the terrible things she'd thought

about Rachel and Kyle at two-thirty this morning. "See you then."

Tia filled her appetizer plate with stuffed mushrooms, shrimp with cocktail sauce, and a beef kabob. Cold vegetables were always the last to go, so she planned to make her return trip to the buffet after she'd taken the edge off her hunger.

At the round table, with her two best friends, Tia waited as they chatted with a good-looking brother from the next table.

The first thing Tia noticed was how clean-cut he was, with his navy suit and white shirt. He'd lost the tie and opened the top collar button, which gave him an air of relaxation in the after-five atmosphere. His hair was neatly edged, and he wore a nice Tag Hauer watch. Tia didn't see a cellular, and she appreciated that. She hated the way Dante worshipped his cell phone. Even when it hadn't rung, he'd looked at it.

Well, that was no longer her worry. His phone had been cut off a few weeks ago, and although she'd given him the money, he'd obviously made another choice. Like finding a new sugar mama.

The stuffed mushrooms in her stomach unstuffed.

"Tia, this is Kirk Giles," Rachel said, with a million-dollar smile. "He's new to Atlanta, from Greenville."

"Welcome," Tia said, realizing Megan's faraway look didn't inspire conversation. "How long have you been here?"

"Six weeks. I'm in broadcasting."

Tia smiled at the unsolicited information. "What type? TV?"

"No, radio. The company I'm with is looking to expand into this market. Your friends mentioned you were in television."

She shrugged. "Weather."

"Maybe we could get together and talk shop sometime."

"Maybe." Tia gave her friends a curious glare, then returned to eating her dinner.

"Can we exchange cards?" he asked, offering his.

Tia hesitated, then gave him her personal card. The last thing she needed was to receive personal calls at work.

"Thanks," she said, having no intention of calling him. He didn't look like her next relationship train wreck, but she hadn't expected to be the lead joke on the evening news either. Life was unexpectedly cruel.

"Have a good evening, ladies," Kirk said as he rose to leave.

With Kirk gone, the trio was left alone.

"He was nice," Megan commented. "You should get with him, Tia."

"At least he has a job," Rachel said, but somehow, coming from her, it sounded insulting.

Tia bit into her last mushroom and chewed, thinking of Fred's rule that when you're really concentrating, nothing can make you angry. She chewed and counted. Did a mental anger check and chewed until she ground her teeth, and there was no more food in her mouth.

Rachel had called this little soirée but didn't seem

to want to get the party started. Her lips were wrapped around the mouth of her second Heineken.

Tia visited the buffet again, ate, then looked Megan in the eye. "Are you crazy?"

Unexpected tears flooded Megan's eyes. "I think so. When I saw his truck, I got to thinking about how many times we'd lain in the bed of the F-150 and dreamed about our future. A space opened up across from his, and before I knew it, I was parked. I didn't expect to see them."

"Why didn't you just leave?" Rachel asked, digging on her plate for a chicken wing.

"I was too shocked. She's got huge boobs. I mean, they're like boulders. Maybe that's why—"

Tia elbowed Megan until she looked at her. "That's not it. Boobs are just . . ." She wanted to say "things" but recalled all too clearly that any time Queen Latifah came on TV, Dante would turn to stone. "They're nothing but big mammary glands that eventually become misshapen and resemble cow teats."

All three cracked up.

"I know it's wrong," Megan admitted. "I shouldn't have been there."

"How'd you find his car, anyway?"

"I just spotted it," Megan said vaguely.

Rachel rolled her eyes. "There are ten thousand parking spaces at the damned airport. If you just happened to luck upon his car, then write down tomorrow's Mega Millions numbers, 'cause you's a lucky bitch."

Tia didn't believe Megan, either. She looked a little off. Her hair was normally pinned up, her make-up Fashion Fair perfect. But today Tia could see her acne scars. And that wasn't Megan.

"Take Megan's hand, Rachel. Promise you won't go near Sonny or his wife again," said Tia.

"He was mine." Megan cried like somebody had died. Or something. Her love for Sonny.

Tia understood. Maybe this was the wake-up call she needed. They'd all dealt with heartbreak differently. She and Dante still had unfinished business, and Rachel had started new business with Kyle.

At the moment, Tia felt like the healthiest of the three, and that wasn't saying much. She'd paid a grand to have her say.

"Look, don't call me when he has you picked up for stalking him," Rachel said, then released Megan's hand and finished her beer.

Megan's head bobbed as she cried softly. "I understand."

"Bullshit," Tia told Rachel. "We're in this together. She's trying to deal with her issues, unlike you, who's spread-eagle and unable to make a sound decision besides blazing blue or neon green condoms."

Rachel's mouth hung open. "No, you didn't! After I took you in."

"Rachel, please. You won't even give me a key," Tia scoffed. "I feel like I'm in boarding school."

Coming around long enough to referee, Megan perked up. "Okay now. Here," Megan said, pouring some of her Heineken into Rachel's bottle. She sopped up what didn't make it into the bottle with her napkin. "Shh, don't say things you don't mean."

"Find somewhere else to board, wench!"

Tia glared at Rachel and twisted her head. "Fine. I will. I've got options." She got off the stool and wobbled a bit. "I'll get my stuff tonight, after I go to the bathroom."

Weaving through the crowd, Tia rejected acknowledging the logical part of her brain that demanded an explanation.

What *options*?

Yeah. Front seat or back.

She passed through a throng of men watching a basketball game when she saw Chance, embroiled in an argument with a woman dressed in an expensive Donna Karan suit. What made the woman stand out was the severe way her hair was pulled off her face and her skillfully applied but dark make-up. Tia was about to go the other way when the woman slapped Chance so hard, her face snapped left, then right.

Stunned, Tia didn't move.

Neither did Chance. She didn't fight or cry or anything. She just stood there.

People around them reacted, but the woman didn't so much as blink at them. She said a few parting words to Chance and left.

Morbid curiosity made Tia watch to see what her bully boss would do, but her bladder begged for relief.

Tia hurried into the ladies' room, and when she got back, Chance was gone.

Megan was at the table by herself when Tia returned.

"This lady just slapped the crap out of Chance."

"Get out."

Adrenaline coursed through Tia. Chance de-

served to get clocked, but without knowing why, Tia
felt a little cheated. Maybe she was the disappointed
lady whose niece Chance hadn't hired yet.

"Where?"

"Over by the bathroom," Tia said.

"Why?"

"I don't know, but if I find out who she is, I'll put
her on my Christmas card list. Where'd Rachel go?"

"Home. She said your things will be on the front
porch."

"Well, that's just perfect!" People around them
turned to stare, and Tia glared back.

"Tia, you're welcome to stay with me, but no, I've
got renovations going on."

Tia patted her friend's hand. "Thanks, sweetie,
but that's okay. I know what I've got to do. Dante is
moving out. Tonight."

Chapter Twelve

Byron rolled into the station parking lot at 6:50 a.m. and parked his cruiser. He was tired, bone weary, as his mother used to say. Too tired to spit.

Before he joined the force, he used to think that working nights was easier than days, but now he knew better, and last night had proven that point.

He'd gotten into a brawl with a pimp when he'd tried to arrest his number one hooker.

The man had been small but quick and had gotten in a couple of good hits. Byron touched his cheek gingerly as he walked into the station.

"Way to go, Rivers. You're sweeping the streets clean single-handedly," one of his fellow officers teased.

Another pointed to his cheek. "Duck next time."

"Funny," Byron responded, taking it in stride. What could he say? He should have ducked.

He flopped down at his desk to sign off on his paperwork before heading home. Lynn wanted to come over to cook, and Byron wanted a good meal but not the pressure that came along with it.

He had too much thinking to do. After the class

the other night, he'd tried to figure out why he hadn't made his presence known to the judge at Tia's hearing. He could have interrupted the dismissal, and she'd have had to answer for escaping from custody.

But poor judgment and sympathy had overridden common sense, and now real concerns about his objectivity plagued him.

After five years on the force and an unblemished record, for the sake of one civilian, he'd jeopardized his job. Could he be objective?

Unable to find a quick resolution, Byron eased into the bustle of ongoing police business and decided that a proactive rather than reactive approach to his career would be best.

"Byron, can you come by my desk, please?" the squad secretary asked.

He waved and started toward Heather, but he was sidetracked by two of the biggest mistakes law enforcement had ever made: Officers Blaire McNult and Joey Rand.

"What's up?" Byron looked for a way to avoid a conversation with them, but no criminals jumped out at him.

"You sure have a way with the women."

McNult, the slightly brighter of the two, demonstrated a level of dimness that surprised Byron and bit off a hangnail, then yelped.

"I'm getting old, gentlemen," Byron told them.

"What're you so wound up for?" Joey demanded. "Found out you didn't pass the detective's exam? I heard only two people passed, so chill."

"That so?" Byron hadn't seen a letter in his mailbox and wondered if he was one of the two or among the many failures. He'd wanted to make detective more than anything. "I've got to get to Heather, fellas. I'll catch up with you later."

Joey hooked his fingers inside his waistband, missing Byron's attempted brush-off. "You know that Samaria King passed." He couldn't hide his look of longing. "She's smart as shit."

Who wouldn't want to be that? Byron thought. The only thing between Joey and a pass at Samaria was her threat to rearrange his face if he ever spoke to her again.

Samaria sat at her desk, accepting accolades.

"And you know that dork, 'call me Calvin, not Cal,' probably passed," Joey went on, "so, you're stuck with us."

Something to look forward to if I go to hell. "Good to know," Byron said. "See you later."

McNult started away, but Joey wasn't done. "We did you a favor, big guy."

Afraid to ask, Byron weighed his options. The two were so stupid that once they'd distributed atheist newsletters at the Baptist church. They'd confided their sin to him one night while on a stakeout. In their younger days, they'd wanted to make an arrest so badly but hadn't wanted to be lucky enough to catch a criminal in the act.

Byron sighed. They weren't going anywhere, so he indulged them. "How did you help me?"

"We arrested a woman who hates you so much, she wants to 'squeeze your neck until your eyes pop out.' That's a direct quote, right, Mc?"

"Right-o."

Tia.

Byron glanced around at the empty desks and conference rooms. "What'd she do?"

"We nabbed her on a B and E, then added threatening an officer," Joey supplied.

"Didn't call her the day after?" McNult asked, with a sneaky grin. "Women want too damned much."

Byron walked down the corridor, his heart racing. All of the interview rooms were empty. He didn't hear or see Tia, and that concerned him. "Where is she?"

Joey jogged alongside, McNult behind. "Holding."

Byron grabbed the keys to his patrol car and picked up the pace. "Was she at a condo on Lenox Road?"

"Yeah. Hey, how'd you know?" Joey couldn't help looking baffled.

"Did you verify her address?"

"No," McNult shot back. "We got a call about a B and E, and we found her. We followed *procedure*. Any questions?"

Byron suppressed the desire to clunk their heads together. "A little investigative work might have turned up a document from Judge Dunn that gave Ms. Amberson permission to reside at the Lenox Road property."

"Shit." McNult coughed and turned red.

The mercury was finally rising. "Has she been booked?" Byron asked.

"No. The victim was on his way"—Joey glanced at his watch—"four hours ago. I dunno." He looked unsure. "Maybe he had to . . . do . . . something."

"I must have skipped the part where *procedure* says we lock up a person and do not press charges."

Byron wouldn't allow himself to feel sorry for them. They were going to catch hell no matter what. "Go talk to the captain."

"Where are you going?" Joey asked, even though McNult punched him in the arm.

"To get her."

"What about the other charge?" Joey wondered aloud.

"Would you shut up?" McNult said and pulled Joey toward the captain's office.

Byron took the stairs down and couldn't imagine what he'd find once he got to holding.

Tia had gone from not ever having had a traffic ticket to having been arrested and locked up twice. She was probably a weeping mess by now.

Byron had to agree with something she'd said to Dr. Khan. If there was ever a person who'd gotten caught up in a bizarre set of circumstances, it was her.

Releasing her would take a little time, but he could at least make her more comfortable upstairs.

Byron entered the holding area and approached the guard station. "Hey, Dave. How's it going?"

"Peachy," he said sarcastically and looked up from his computer. "We got a singer. Driving everybody nuts."

"That bad, huh?"

"Can't wait for that one to fall asleep. Who you here for?"

"Tia Amberson. She's going to be released in about an hour. Case of mistaken, uh, arrest."

"I'll do you one better." The older black man snatched papers from the printer, assembled them in a folder, and handed it all to Byron. "Been waitin' to hand this off since she got here. Everything you need is right there. Go on. Get her now."

Suddenly, Byron wasn't eager to go in back. "Why?"

"You can't miss her. She's the one with all the noise coming out of her mouth. See ya later, good-bye, and good luck."

Dave buzzed Byron through. After the first door automatically closed, another buzzer and a series of doors led him into the inner sanctum of holding, where he was slapped across the face by the worst kind of off-key singing he'd ever heard.

Surely, that wasn't Tia.

"Nobody knows the trouble I see, nobody knows but me-eeee. Nobody knows the trouble I see, nobody knows but me-eeee.

"No justice, no peace. No justice, no peace."

Not the picket sign chant.

Byron looked at Officer Howard, who had a firm grip on his can of pepper spray. "How long has she been at it?"

"Two hours, twenty-three minutes, and ten seconds. God, she's awful. Make her shut up, and I'll give you my tickets to the next Hawks game."

"That's nice of you, man, but keep the tickets. Take your wife."

"My wife sings worse than her. That's the only thing that stopped me from giving the lady back there a gullet full of pepper spray."

Byron walked through the holding area, passing women in various stages of distress. The most aggravated of them stood at the front of their cells. "Shut her up!"

"Shoot 'er now!"

"If she starts that song again, I'll hang myself!"

Officer Howard gestured Byron forward while he worked on quieting the other inmates.

Tia sat on the floor of her empty cell, her back against the bed, her knees drawn up. She didn't even acknowledge Byron as he entered the steel cage.

"Nobody knows—"

"Tia, your arrest was a misunderstanding. The charges have been dropped."

"The trouble—"

"Tia, do you hear me?"

"Swing loooow, sweet chariot . . ."

A lady in the next cell screamed loud and long and started throwing whatever she could get her hands on.

Byron crouched down. "Tia? You're acting ridiculous."

She looked tired, but her eyes, void of liner and shadow, were angry. "Get out of my room."

He reached for her. "The charges were dropped."

"I'm not leaving."

Crashing commenced behind him. An inmate revolt? Oh, hell, no. "Tia, you have to leave."

"Or what? I'll be locked up on not leaving jail charges?" Her maniacal laughter concerned him. Obviously, her interaction with Atlanta's finest had sent her over the edge.

He searched for something positive to say. "I'm sorry about the misunderstanding." Shoes hit the steel bars behind him, and screaming moved toward them like a clawed tiger. "And on behalf of the officers, I want to, uh, formally apologize for the department and have you released within the hour."

Tia crossed her arms. "This is grand, considering I didn't belong here in the first place."

"Tia, you vandalized—"

"I owned the tires!"

Byron started to agree for the sake of peace. "That's an arguable point, but—"

"But Mutt and Jeff wouldn't listen."

Joey and McNult stood outside Tia's cell, the raving women on both sides making them nervous.

"Nobody would listen to me, not even you," she told Byron. "So if there's no justice for me, then there's no peace for you. Swing loooow, sweet chariot . . ."

Mattresses flew, and women started beating the crap out of each other.

Byron did the only logical thing. He tossed Tia neatly over his shoulder.

She kicked, her foot landing near his crown jewels, and he gave her a whack on the rear. "Kick one more time, and I'll feed you to the lions."

He capitalized on her momentary paralysis and ran for their lives.

Chapter Thirteen

In the parking lot, Tia scrambled out of Byron's arms and wiped her hands over herself. "How dare you manhandle me? Don't ever touch me again!"

"Fine."

"Fine!"

He had the nerve to keep himself between her and the station, as if he was in charge of weeding out the real criminals from the fake.

How many people had ever been uninvited to jail?

Tears filled her eyes at yet another bizarre happening in her life. Fate was kicking her ass right about now.

Close to crying, Tia sucked in a cold breath and tried to get her bearings. Second Street? She was at least one and a half miles from work, and she only had a half hour to get to her desk.

She started down the long driveway, heading toward the street. Maybe she could flag a cab or catch a bus that would put her close to the building.

She raised her arm and the taxi driver gestured

up. He was off duty. Pulling her arms close to her body to conserve heat, Tia started walking.

"I've been ordered to escort you home. If you wait a minute, I'll get the car and drive you home. We can deal with Manuel right now," Byron snarled.

"I *never* want to see you again."

"Tia—"

"I'd rather stay in jail." She circled and Byron blocked her and Tia went the other way.

"You made that clear," he said, as officers ran past them and into the building.

She snatched her purse from him and walked faster.

Byron couldn't believe her. "Where are you going?"

"Anywhere you're not."

He thought of letting her go alone, but what if she got hit by a car or died of hypothermia? He'd be blamed for not following orders.

Then *he'd* be in jail. "You don't want a ride. Fine with me. I'm still going to do my job."

She kept walking.

Hurrying back to his squad car, Byron trailed her for a block, flashers on, the stares from passersby almost as ridiculous as her walking in the thirty-degree weather.

They looked as if they were having a lovers' quarrel. On PD time.

Tia was creating a hazardous situation. He could arrest her, or leave her alone. Now that was a plan.

He radioed his captain.

"What is it, Rivers?" Hanks was angry, but there *was* a riot in his jail. Ever since their run-in, they'd kept a respectful distance. Byron was aware that everyone knew that Hanks was under investigation because of him, but he didn't rub it in the man's face. All Byron wanted was respect for himself and his fellow officers, and to his credit, Hanks had calmed down, a bit. But this call might change everything.

"State your business, Officer."

"Ms. Amberson refuses a ride. I'll return to the station now."

"Oh no, you don't."

Tia crossed the street, and Byron stomped on the brakes. Horns blared behind him. He gritted his teeth and U-turned in the middle of the street. "What am I supposed to do? Arrest her?"

"Don't even think about it," Hanks snapped. "I was just told her coat is still here. Is that true?"

Thin silk showcased the lines of a sexy black bra and a smooth back. He cleared his throat. "Yes, sir."

"Officer Rivers, if Ms. Amberson so much as catches a head cold and we get sued, you'll be held personally responsible. Deal with her!"

There were terrorists to be caught, and what was he doing? Following an ill-tempered woman who'd rather march around with no coat than take a free ride.

"And don't think just because you passed the detective's exam, that will stop me from seeing you in the unemployment line."

Byron's heart rejoiced. He'd made it. "You won't have the chance, sir," he said with pride.

"Then we have an understanding. You have to successfully complete the anger management course and get it signed off by me."

"I'll do whatever is necessary to earn my promotion."

"You're catching on. You can start by adhering to the judge's order and making sure Ms. Amberson takes possession of her home."

Life was nothing but a spring-loaded mousetrap. He swallowed a heavy sigh. "Yes, sir."

"Rivers?"

"Sir?" Byron said.

"I consider it your personal responsibility to see that Tia Amberson never enters my precinct again."

Byron didn't say that he thought it was more likely for him to get a job on the space station.

Tia turned the corner and crossed the street. Now her arms were folded over her middle, with her head dipped toward her chest. She had to be freezing.

"You can count on me, sir," Byron said and disconnected the call.

The snarl of traffic behind his patrol car grew longer.

With Tia marching along as the lone soldier, Byron knew he'd have to be an officer of his word.

He pulled into the parking lot of a nearby building, yanked on his jacket, and retrieved a blanket from the trunk.

He started off on foot and caught up to Tia. Sure enough, she was shivering, but she didn't stop walking. That'd be too easy.

He draped her shoulders and prepared for the blanket to hit the pavement. When it didn't, he fell into step beside her.

"You have two choices," he told her.

"Is that your standard pickup line?"

Byron couldn't help but laugh. "Who said anything about picking you up? Who'd want to? You're a hostile, volatile woman."

"So I've been told by all the men I've encountered this past month."

Tia jaywalked and horns blared.

Byron caught her by the arm. "Are you trying to be roadkill?"

"No, but I was hoping my stalker might."

"You're a smart-ass, you know that?"

She kept walking.

His temper tipped the scale. "*Now* you don't have anything to say? While you were causing a riot and a traffic jam, you couldn't keep your mouth shut. The judge said for me to escort you. Why didn't you just call?"

Tia stood in stony silence at the light and began to cross with the other pedestrians.

"Unbelievable!" Byron's foot crunched against litter, the shine on his shoe marred with every furious step.

He'd arrested fourteen prostitutes and pimps over the past four days, but Tia's brief yet memorable incarceration would be all he heard about, possibly for the rest of his career. They walked down Peachtree Street, toward the Fox Theatre marquee glittering on their left. At the corner they crossed, and his nose perked up the scent of brewing coffee and scrambled eggs when two women balancing Styrofoam containers and coffee cups stepped outside the diner.

His stomach yelped like an excited puppy. At this hour of the morning he would have had a light dinner and been in his bed. But twelve hours of hard police work wasn't enough. He had to baby-sit.

She turned then, the depth of her anger etched down the center of her face. "I'm tired of being told what to do. Everybody else lives by their own rules, but I have to ask permission. Last night I didn't have anywhere else to go. I just wanted to go home. And I didn't want to ask you to take me there."

Pedestrians streamed past, staring openly.

"People live within the law, Tia. When they don't, that's when Atlanta PD steps in."

The reprimand fell on deaf ears as the crowd mobilized, herding them across the street. Byron picked up the pace as Tia power-walked around other pedestrians. Several times he dropped back to let people traveling south the opportunity to pass, but the distance between him and Tia grew.

She walked on oblivious of him, like she had been since they'd met. He wasn't sure he liked that, given that many of his thoughts centered around her. "Step to the left. Left. Left," he said, directing the comment to three women whose looks said they didn't give a damn who he was, they weren't moving.

The shoulder of a blonde woman brushed his, but she didn't break stride.

"Watch it," he ordered, to which she responded by flipping him the backward bird.

What happened to respect for the damned law?

Pissed, Byron caught up to Tia and grasped her shoulder just as her foot left the curb to jaywalk. "Enough," he said, and she stopped.

He tried to ignore that she bumped his hand off

her shoulder with a shrug. "Let's get him out of your house now."

Misery collapsed her features and she looked like she was going to cry. "I can't."

Was this another game? He could hear the sympathy symphony start rehearsals. With every curse word he thought, her face changed to a darker, angrier Tia. How many levels did this woman possess?

"After all you've been through, you didn't just say no. I didn't hear that."

He looked into her eyes and saw the truth. "What the hell is it now, Tia?"

"I'm in trouble at work. If I'm late or don't show up, I'm fired. Here's your blanket."

Wind skittered up Peachtree, scattering debris around their ankles. Byron noticed a lone maintenance man wrestling a broken bag of garbage, hunkered down in his blue quilt jacket, losing the battle, terribly.

Byron held the blanket helplessly, not wanting to yield. Wanting to sleep. With her, he realized, with surprising clarity. Not with Lynn, but with the difficult yet beautiful woman an arm's length away.

He urged Tia to the door of the building. "I'll explain to your boss you have urgent business to attend to."

She spun out of his hold and headed back to the cold street. Chill bumps raced over her chest and up to her cheeks. He wanted to kiss her, but instead, he held her close.

"No."

His desire ratcheted up in degrees. "You don't have a choice—"

"She won't care! She wants to fire me. She's practically given my job away. Without a job, I have no home—considering I don't have it anyway, I don't have too far to go before I'm the best dressed woman on skid row. Then I'm going to need a house! This crappy piece of a job is all I have, and I can't screw that up, too."

Her gaze flew toward the busy traffic and he wondered if she was planning to end it all right here, right now.

She wouldn't. Not because the thought hadn't occurred to her, but because he wasn't a lucky man.

Tia started toward another door, her lower jaw trembling.

He wasn't sure if from the cold or her burst of helpless anger, although it didn't matter. He was going to bed before noon, even if he had to cuff her to the steering wheel in his car to do it.

Tia started inside and Byron blocked her. "We have to leave."

"Please," she pleaded. "Go away, I don't want my boss to see you."

"Dammit. You're coming with me."

"No! No! No, I'm not!"

Everyone within a five-foot radius stopped walking, aimed their cell phones, and pressed record. Every citizen was, after all, one event away from being on *The Today Show.*

"Hold on." Byron let her go, holding up his hands to show no police brutality was taking place. "Let's talk calmly."

"I am calm," she said, her jaw jutting. "You're trying to bully me and I won't have it."

"That's not true. We just have two different agendas," he said agreeably, as the cameras continued to record. "What do you propose?"

"I'll go to work, and we go to my condo as soon as I get off."

That was eight hours from now. Plenty of time for Tia to find trouble and dive in. If Hanks found out Byron disobeyed orders, no amount of pimp and prostitute arrests would save him. His career rested on this decision.

He'd made detective. No more uniform. No more McNult and Joey. No more Captain Hanks. He had too damned much to lose. "I can't."

Byron guided her away from the building by the hand without any resistance. He felt as if he were leading a toddler away from the big swings.

"Are you going to hit her?" a disappointed man asked, his camera phone pointing at himself, then Byron for the impromptu interview.

"No, sir. I'm only offering aid."

The man snapped his phone shut and muttered foul language at Byron for wasting his time.

Byron tugged Tia's hand as she lagged. When he turned to look at her, his heart flipped over.

She was crying. Tears fell in great big drops off her chin. She covered her eyes and yielded to the flood of emotion.

"I'm following orders. Don't do this." The wind carried his plea into the street and dumped it in front of a swift-moving M.A.R.T.A. bus.

Byron felt crazy as people stared at Tia and the mean police officer with the blanket in his hands. He hurriedly put it around her shoulders and in the process, brought her against his chest. He tucked the blanket around her, his resistance being clobbered by her femininity. Tia fit against him in that oh so perfect way no woman had ever done before. He tried to remain Byron, officer of law and order, but with her in his arms he was slowly slipping into Byron, the man. And Byron the man couldn't resist a vulnerable Tia.

His lips slid across her cheek, and the dampness of her tears moistened them.

He began to groan and realized it was a croon meant to soothe her. Without words he tried to restore her peace. And for just a few minutes she let him.

When she won the struggle with her emotions, she pushed away from him. "I promise to behave all day. We can pick up fighting later, I promise."

Despite himself, he chuckled. She shivered and even through his Kevlar vest, he felt the impact all the way to his bones.

"Do you know how much trouble you are? Do you realize everything I've worked my entire professional career for is on the line?"

Talk about making a bargain with the devil. He had to hand it to her. She was the prettiest devil he'd ever laid eyes on. A sigh built in his chest, and he let it go.

Tears tipped her long black eyelashes, and he wanted to rub them away.

"Cut off the waterworks because it doesn't affect me. I have four sisters." Another tear slid down, and God help him, he wiped it away. "Not an ounce of trouble," he warned. "If there's a fire alarm, a heart attack, or a car crash within a mile of this building, I'm arresting you."

Relief swept her face into its most innocent state. The lines of fatigue and the tint of darkness vanished, leaving the nakedness of a sincere woman. Again, his chest clenched. All he could think about was being inside her.

"I promise."

"Tia, is this officer giving you a hard time?"

A white, scrawny, cross-dressing man stared at him. He sounded like a woman, but it was clear that under the wig and make-up, the pencil leg pants and wedged shoes, was an Adam, not an Eve.

"Not really, Rhonda/Ronnie. Byron, do we have an agreement?"

"Tia—" Byron groaned.

The cross-dresser circled them. "What's the problem? Maybe Rhonda/Ronnie can help."

"Officer Rivers has informed me that I need to take possession of my condo right now."

"You can't, Tia." Rhonda/Ronnie grew animated. "I saw Chance the dragon slayer about an hour ago, and she's on a tear. And she'd love to rip you a new one." Rhonda/Ronnie leaned in. "Between us, if you go into work looking like a mangled Stepford Wife, you won't keep the job you barely have."

"Thank you, Rhonda/Ronnie," Tia said dryly. Her gaze met Byron's. "I won't do one bad thing today. Please trust me."

It was hard for Byron to look away because he missed looking into Tia's eyes. He shook his head at what he was about to do.

"Five o'clock, and not a minute—"

Before he could finish, Tia wrapped her arms around his neck and pressed her lips into his cheek. "Thank you."

Instinctively he turned his mouth to her and looked into her smoldering eyes. Tia stepped back.

The cold wind moved in as she backed away. "I'll be right here at five o'clock."

Rhonda/Ronnie took Tia's hand and guided her toward the corner. "Come on, Peacock. We've got to hurry. I've got some make-up and a shirt that just might fit you."

Byron watched until they disappeared inside the building.

Wind blasted him out of his stupor, and he wondered if he'd just committed professional suicide.

Chapter Fourteen

Tia hurried behind Ronnie/Rhonda, who used a pass code to enter doors Tia had never paid attention to before. "Where are you taking me?"

"To find some clothes you didn't have on yesterday. Honey, if I noticed, everyone will. Now be quiet, and let Rhonda/Ronnie do her thing."

Rhonda/Ronnie had insulted her in that breezy way gay men had turned into an art form, but Tia could hardly argue. She did smell like the bottom of somebody's foot.

At the far left corner, Rhonda/Ronnie tapped in his code, and they entered the make-up room, where the newscasters got prepped for the newscasts.

Tia ran her hand along red leather salon chairs, her heart wistful. Once upon a time, she had expected to spend a lot of time in here, reviewing her notes before going live on the air, but somewhere along the way, she'd jacked up her karma. And riding a desk on the disintegrating thread of a performance review was all she was capable of at the moment.

But, still, she felt like she belonged in this room. In this job.

Gently touching a rolling rack of tops and jackets for both men and women, Tia wandered back to the chairs in front of the lighted mirrors. Sitting, she swiveled.

Rhonda/Ronnie opened a drawer beneath the mirrors and pulled out a new bag of men's Hanes briefs, ripped the plastic, and handed Tia a pair.

"What are these for?"

"Honey, funky doesn't become you."

Embarrassment crept over Tia like a tidal wave. "I had a hard night. I didn't get home, and . . ." She could feel the tears coming. "I'm not myself today. Why am I putting you to all this trouble? If Chance sees me, I'm done." Wearily, her arms fell to her sides as tears stung the back of her eyes.

"Peacock, you can't let her win by default. Seize the opportunity to be the hero in your own life, and then tell the story. Like why you smell like the inside of a jail. I'd also like to know the identity of the hunky guy you were wrapped around outside."

"I was not."

"If you'd had a bed . . ." Rhonda/Ronnie began to sing to the tune of "If I didn't care."

"Quit. He's someone—"

"Yes, he is," Rhonda/Ronnie agreed, with an appreciative little bark.

"I met in anger management class."

"Ooh. Is he angry, too? Does he get all snarly and rough, get your hands behind your back?" Rhonda/Ronnie said, imitating a cop in a falsetto voice. "Don't make me frisk you."

Tia couldn't help but laugh as Rhonda ran his hands all over himself on Byron's behalf.

"I don't think that's the highlight of his day."

"Would be of mine! I'd make it his."

"Ronnie!"

"I'm Rhonda today. My Sean Johns didn't come back from the cleaners yesterday like they were supposed to."

"Sorry."

Rhonda really did like men *and* women. That shouldn't have surprised Tia. Rhonda's T-shirt said THE BOY IS MINE.

"One last question before you go wash up."

Tia indulged her new best friend. "What is it?"

"Do you think he'd ever take a trip to Down Low Boulevard?"

Of all the things Tia'd thought of Byron, being a closet bisexual wasn't one of them. The idea of it made her stomach rumble. The truth was that although she'd been angry with him more than she'd been with any man besides Dante, there was an attraction there. And it was definitely mutual, and definitely hetero.

"Rhonda, if I didn't consider you my best friend at this moment, I'd strangle you."

She cocked her hip to the side. "Coulda said he was taken, *Gawd.* Violence ain't cute, because there's plenty of Ms. Rodmans out there. Now, you'd better get a move on. You have just enough time to take a five-minute shower and get your new undies on, and ten minutes for me to do something wicked with your hair. Now shoo."

Tia started away but turned back. "Why are

you doing this for me? I don't want you to get into any trouble."

"Don't worry about me, doll. I'll be fine."

"But Chance—" Tia stopped.

"Yes?" He fingered a few of the shirts on the rack. "You can speak freely. Nothing said will go out of this room. You think she's a bitch?"

Tia gazed up at Rhonda/Ronnie from the other end of the rack. Although they were brother and sister, Tia would never have been able to tell by the way they acted. Rhonda/Ronnie was invisible to Chance, which was unfortunate. Ronnie was a great man.

"Chance doesn't like me, and I can get used to that, but penalizing me for sick time I earned is wrong. I heard her promising my job to someone over the phone the other day, but she has to get rid of me first. I won't just walk away or knowingly give her a reason."

Tia shrugged. "I just won't. I'll get through this, whatever the outcome. I just don't want you to get into trouble because of me."

Beneath all the make up, Rhonda/Ronnie's face softened. "I'm helping you because you're one of the good guys," he said, in his natural voice. "Chop-chop, Peacock. The bewitching hour is near."

Tia touched her face as she hustled up two flights of stairs to the fourteenth floor. Rhonda/Ronnie had given her the makeover of the century. Tia barely recognized herself, yet the spike in her self-esteem was short-lived when she saw she was sixty-eight seconds late for work.

Rhonda/Ronnie stopped ahead of her, doorknob in hand. "Don't fold under pressure. Tell her the elevator was stuck and that she can get a repair log from maintenance."

"Why delay the inevitable? She's going to find out that's a lie."

Rhonda/Ronnie shushed her. "Not if you let me work my magic. You look good. Now go."

Tia entered the floor and stopped short. "Mr. And Mrs. Norman," she said, greeting the station owners. "How nice to see you."

The door behind Tia banged shut. She could hear Rhonda/Ronnie taking the stairs down two at a time.

"Tia! You look amazing," Mrs. Norman exclaimed. "What have you done to yourself? The colors you've put together are wonderful."

"It's nothing," Tia said, swallowing. "Something I threw together at the last minute."

"Winton, doesn't she look great?"

"Yes, Maylene. I told you long ago she had 'the look' to be on-air talent. Tia, have you given any more thought to being on camera?"

Had she? That was her dream come true.

"As a matter of fact—"

"You're late."

The ice-cold reprimand pushed Tia to the threshold of panic, where she teetered. "Good morning, Chance." She greeted the bristly woman with a smile. "I was just saying hello to your folks."

"Darling," Maylene said to her daughter. "Is that how you greet everyone?"

"Mother, Tia is on an action plan for attendance."

"I thought that was over."

Tia regarded Chance, with vengeance in her heart. She'd led Tia to believe the Normans had agreed to this ridiculous punishment. And since she'd signed off on the action plan, she had no recourse but to follow through, and Tia wasn't going to make it easy for Chance to steal her job.

"You're one tough cookie, and that's what we like. But, Chance." Mrs, Norman touched her daughter's wrist, which seemed to move by remote up her jacket sleeve, leaving Mrs. Norman little choice but to stop touching her. "It hardly seems fair to penalize Tia when we were chatting with her. Right, Winton?"

Mr. Norman had gone into a nearby cube and was at the computer, involved in a spreadsheet. "That's right. We have meetings, Maylene. Chance?"

"Yes?" Chance glanced over her shoulder to see if anyone was listening and gave Tia the evil eye. "What is it?"

"You're looking more corpse-like than usual. You need more vitamin C in your diet, and some ultra-violet rays wouldn't hurt. Come up later, and I'll give you a handful of my vitamins. Can't do anything about you getting more sun, though."

There was a God, Tia thought, sucking her lips in so she wouldn't laugh. Chance looked mortified, as her cheeks took on a pinkish hue. Like when the woman slapped her. Tia still couldn't erase that picture from her mind.

"Mother, Father," she said through clenched teeth. "I don't want to keep you from your meetings, so you'd better run along."

"You're right, of course. Tia, so great to see you." Mrs. Norman enveloped her in a cloud of Estee

Lauder. "You look great. Those colors . . . I don't know, that outfit looks familiar, yet different."

Tia started a slow slide backward. She didn't want Mrs. Norman, the self-professed queen of Nordstrom, to connect that the anchors sometimes wore these clothes on TV!

"You know how it is when you shop at T.J. Maxx," said Tia. "One person's designer is another person's bargain. Good to see you. Let's talk again soon."

"Right, dear. Chance," her mother cooed, "walk us out."

Chance's look said she wasn't going to let Tia get away with anything.

Tia felt like she'd been the beneficiary of two miracles today. Perhaps her good luck had returned. She rounded the corner of her workstation and prayed Chance would get locked in the elevator.

At her desk, she poured four broken Tums into her hand and chewed one at a time. Down to the last pieces, Tia wondered how she'd survive the next week and a half until payday.

She'd be home tonight, and if Dante hadn't eaten everything, she'd have her first real hot meal in days.

But the likelihood of him leaving her food was slim and none.

She needed money. She pulled out her checkbook register and read the entries for the past month. *Macy's, Quik Trip gas, Kroger, insurance, Coach store, Dillard's, package store* (She needed her weekly bottle of Pinot Grigio.) *Café Lisette's, Publix, Coach store for the matching wallet, Kroger, BP gas, Macy's, Kroger, Chanel, Nordstrom, eBay, Publix, car note.*

Tia racked her brain. She'd bought a lot of groceries last month for someone with no food. She flipped back to the prior month and noticed the same thirty-dollar withdrawal, in addition to larger entries for Kroger.

The months preceding indicated the same. It finally struck her. *Birth control pills.*

Her hand hovered over the phone as she contemplated. If she went off the pill for a couple of months, that would save her sixty dollars, money she desperately needed right now. She could buy the generic antacid and still have enough money left over to pay for her overdue car tag. Or she could buy groceries.

"Tia."

She heard her name whispered but didn't see anyone.

She popped another Tums, sad that she was almost through with breakfast. "Yeah?"

"Want to buy a candy bar from my daughter? She's trying to go to band camp. Forty-six boxes of this crap we have to sell."

That was Victor Nash. The man had six kids, a wife, and provided for them on forty-six thousand dollars a year. On principle alone, Tia tried to help when she could.

She started to decline but stopped short. "Vic, what'd you bring for lunch?"

"Roast beef on rye."

"Fruit?"

"Yeah, an apple. Why?"

"How much is the candy?"

"Two-fifty a pop."

Excited, she scrounged in her desk and came up with two dollars and eighty-three cents. Tia dropped the extra change back into the drawer. She might need that for another lunch. "I'll buy one bar if you give me your lunch, too."

"What! I'll be hungry by lunchtime."

"You've got more roast beef at home, man. But can you eat forty-six boxes of chocolate?"

"Crap," he whispered. "Fine."

Vic shuffled over, took the money, and dropped the candy and his lunch on her desk. "You the black Mafia now?"

"Get out," she told him, with a smile.

She devoured half the sandwich in a few bites, then forced herself to stop.

Two dollars and fifty cents had bought her three meals today. She didn't want to eat them all in one sitting.

Tia dialed the mail room to tell Rhonda/Ronnie she was still employed but was told she'd been called into a meeting with the Normans.

The roast beef and rye staged a revolt, but Tia coated her stomach with two more precious Tums and prayed her new best friend wasn't in trouble because of her.

The clock read 9:30. She'd had the morning from hell, but things were hopefully looking up.

Byron's face popped into her mind. He'd been stern and angry, but when she left him, his eyes had been wary. Behind them, though, had been something else. Longing, she realized. Did he have a woman? Definitely not. Who'd have a hard-ass like him?

Tia flicked the computer mouse back and forth idly. He'd rescued her again. Was there a limit to how many times a person could be saved by one police officer?

She didn't think so but bargained that if she made it through the day without getting fired, *and* got the condo without any drama, she'd kiss Byron Rivers on the mouth.

In 2065.

By the time Tia walked through the revolving doors of Colony Square, the sky was dark, winter showing off its power. Cold air braced Tia on each side, and she hesitated, wishing her next steps were to the destiny of her choosing. Except her chauffeur-driven squad car was waiting.

Byron stepped out and came around just as she reached for the handle. "You can't sit in the front," he said.

Tia sucked her teeth, attitude enveloping her like the cold wind. "Do I have to look like I'm under arrest as I leave the job I barely have?"

"Why is everything always a fight with you?"

"Back in trouble again, Tia? This is so you . . . so perfect." Chance had walked up behind Tia, catching her off guard.

The smirk on her face stung to the soles of Tia's aching feet. Her mother had always taught her that hate wasn't possible if love lived in a person's heart, but that was another lie Millicent Amberson had passed on to her gullible child.

Tia's purse slid down the sleeve of her borrowed jacket. Screw the rest-of-her-life list. Kicking Chance's ass was the only thing she had left to do before she died. "Chance, I've had it—"

"Tia, we have to get going if we're going to make it to our dinner reservations on time."

Byron's arm slid around Tia's neck in a semi-choke hold.

"You're"—Chance looked off into the distance for the answer to her assumption—"you're not here to arrest her?"

"Why would I do that?"

"Because she's guilty of a crime?" Chance said, as if Byron were the biggest doofus in the world.

"I don't usually incarcerate my dates. We're late, darlin'," he said to Tia.

He'd only planned to peck her on the lips, but after this morning's nonsense and his midmorning dreams, he couldn't help kissing Tia for real. All day he'd felt anxious, until now.

He took her into his arms and let their mouths touch. Slowly, her soft lips slid against his, and when the delicate tip of her tongue greeted his, Byron knew this was no longer playacting. He let his guard down and enjoyed the moment.

When their mouths finally separated, he realized her scary-looking boss was still there. "Good night," he told her.

Byron opened the passenger door and helped Tia inside. She glanced up at Chance, who had turned a lovely shade of stupid, and rolled her eyes.

When Byron climbed inside and shifted the car into drive, Tia kissed him again, her fingers playing at the base of his scalp. His cheek tingled.

"Is she still looking?" he said, his voice heavy until he cleared his throat.

"Yep." Tia watched through the passenger rearview mirror.

"She's a piece of work."

"Her jaw is still on the ground. She's Cruella De Vil, black heart included."

Byron drove around the corner and merged into evening traffic, the bright red and white lights from other cars winking at them.

Tia yawned, lack of sleep catching up to her. Although her heart pounded and her eyes begged to close, she couldn't really rest until she was inside her home.

She gazed at him and couldn't look away. She noticed the strength of his jaw, the curve of his full lips, and the way he gripped the steering wheel in his large, capable hands. Tia blinked, feeling things she had no right to. "I owe you. Thank you."

"Just doing my job."

Inexplicably, the statement rubbed her like sandpaper against raw skin. "Is everything with you about your job?"

"You trying to say I don't have a life?"

"I'm asking if you do."

"Yes, I have a life."

"No elaboration? 'Yes, I do,'" Tia imitated. "You just seem like you could be, and I'm not saying that you are, but boring."

"Is that so?" He smiled, and his dimple winked at her. She wanted to stick her tongue in the little indent.

"Yes. What do you do for fun?" Tia asked, needing to know more about the man that had insinuated himself so intricately into her life.

"I have fun, and it's none of your business."

"Good answer," she said softly. "You just had your tongue in my mouth, and I shouldn't know what you do to have fun?" Tia giggled and squeezed his

right leg. The muscle jumped against her palm.
"Talk about putting the cart before the horse."

She pulled her hand away and looked out the
passenger window. "You hide behind your job. I
said thank you. A simple 'you're welcome' would
have sufficed."

He looked at her, then back at the road.

"Thank you, Byron," she said pointedly.

He breathed deeply and shook his head. "You're
welcome."

Tia folded her arms. "That wasn't so hard, was it?
So," she said, glancing out the passenger window,
enjoying the familiar scenery, "what do you do
when you're not working? You a member of the
stun gun club?"

"You are not funny," he said, although he smiled
a little. "Once you're in the house, you should consider changing the locks."

He'd successfully averted any conversation about
himself, returning to the reason why she was in his
car. She'd tried to even the playing field, yes, for
her own comfort, but he wasn't having it.

"I'll take that under consideration," was all Tia
could manage through tight lips.

He glanced at her before bringing the squad car
to a smooth stop.

"Have you been patrolling the condo parking lot
since our unfortunate meeting?"

"No. My zone was changed."

"Because of me?"

"The 22,400 people that live in zone two needed
another patrol car added for their protection.
Nothing to do with you. Sorry."

"Oh." Acute embarrassment knocked on the door

of her ego and gave her a fat lip. Life, as he'd so eloquently mentioned, wasn't all about her. So why did she feel as if she were under a hot microscope?

"I was just wondering if you'd seen anything out of the ordinary?"

"No, but you're not expecting anything strange to happen, are you?"

Strange? Tia didn't know how to answer that. *Dumped. Jailed. Deserted by her one loyal best friend. Potentially losing her job.*

Tia wasn't sure, but she didn't think things could get any more bizarre. "No."

"Have you had any encounters with your ex?"

"No, I haven't seen Dante, or talked to or thought about him, except about how much pleasure I'm going to have when I squash him like the little bug that he is."

The car jerked, and Tia lurched forward, her hands smacking the dashboard as cars screeched to a halt behind them.

"Have you forgotten how to drive?" she sniped. "I just did twenty-four hours in jail. I don't want my last thought to be, is my mother going to get my coffin at a closeout sale on the Internet?"

Disbelief skittered across his face, and Tia knew she'd just made another mistake.

"This is a camera light," he said with force. "I have to obey the laws like everyone else." Byron jabbed his finger at her, then the light. "But that's beside the point. You must have enjoyed your stay in jail, because you just made a threat against a man you've been ordered to stay away from. You're talking to a police officer, for God's sake."

"I may be, but I'm also talking to a man with four

sisters. You should know when we're talking junk and when we're not. Besides, Byron, in the same situation any one of them could have been me."

He really laughed then. Tia considered wringing his neck, but then she wouldn't be a visitor in prison, but a resident.

She shoved her hands under her thighs.

"My sisters would never threaten to take out their ex-lovers. They're all upstanding citizens, as you should be."

"After what I've been through, I should be able to get a taste of revenge. An eye for an eye. You've heard of it."

"Don't try to get me to agree with your sick philosophy." He was quiet for a moment. "What are you planning?" Byron demanded.

"None of your business."

"You're done with him. He's gone. You're getting your house back, and pretty soon your life will return to whatever normal is for you. Why would you want to risk freedom for revenge? Is he worth it?"

Tia didn't say that she wanted to hurt Dante for hurting her, because these emotions were new. All her life she'd always been the calm one. Always in control. But now all she could think about was rocking his greasy-headed boat. In the deep sad recesses of her heart, she wanted to examine what had happened to their relationship. But then the reasonable woman inside her wanted to leave the past behind— after she got him back.

Still, Byron's points were valid. Her life was inside that house around the corner, and she could start over.

"You're right. He's not worth it."

Byron patted her knee, leaving a memorable handprint. "No, he isn't. Get in the house. Deal with your personal issues and move on."

Byron eased the car onto the property and drove slowly.

Any rebuttal Tia wanted to make was swallowed in the familiarity of being so close to home. The stoop looked lonely without the huge pots of petunias she'd planted last year to add an inviting splash of color. Each day when she'd left the house, she'd smile at the blooms, and upon her return every evening, it was as if the flowers were welcoming her home. Tomorrow she'd put the pots out even though it was too soon for the flowers. That would show the world that the ugly smudge their breakup had left on the neighborhood was being erased. It would signal that she was moving forward.

She'd hung the sea green shears over the single-pane clear glass side panels on either side of the front door four weeks ago, her dream of a serene entryway to the house falling apart with the breakup. Decorating had been her focus all those weeks ago. Making the relationship work had been important.

Now the thought of seeing Dante again made her stomach squeeze.

Byron parked next to the handicap spaces and got out. Coming around, he opened her door, offering her his hand.

Tia thought of leaving him hanging but didn't. Just because she felt evil didn't mean she had to be evil. Besides, he'd be out of her life soon, too.

Stepping out of the car, she eased ahead of Byron and walked up the short flight of stairs, her heart thundering.

"You got your keys?" he asked.

"I do."

Tia inserted the key and was attempting to turn it when the door was wrenched open.

She backed up, surprised at the black woman who stood before her, clad in a floral silk robe, curly weave cascading down both sides of her face. She was thick, her lipstick faded, her mouth twisted at being disturbed.

"Who the hell are you?" Tia demanded.

"The new tenant, Ida Wilkes. I heard you might be stopping by. This is for you."

The woman shoved a sheaf of papers into Tia's hand.

Incomprehension flooded her as she stared at them. Lease agreement? What the hell?

"There must be some kind of misunderstanding," Tia said. "This is my home."

The woman cocked her head. "*You* would be the one not understanding. You see, you might own it, but I rented it. This lease agreement says so. Buh-bye."

Rage suffused Tia, and before she could think through her actions, she launched herself through the closing door, caught a handful of hair, and yanked.

Chapter Fifteen

In the back of the squad car, Tia wiped her tears. Byron was glad that he hadn't cuffed her, after the unexpected attack on Ms. Wilkes.

"I want that crazy bitch arrested!" Ida Wilkes stood on the stoop outside, holding her head, pointing at Tia. "She yanked out my weave. She assaulted me!"

"She thought your hair was going to close in the door. She was trying to help you." *Great lie*, and so far from the truth, Byron had a hard time keeping a straight face. Hair streamed through Ms. Wilkes's fingers, a whole section of French braids visible on her scalp.

"What the hell kind of excuse is that?"

"I can't account for her logic." Byron looked back at Tia, who was unrepentant and hollering in the car. "Who leased you this condo?" he asked Ida Wilkes.

"The former owner, Dante Manuel."

"He's not the rightful owner. Ms. Amberson is."

"Mr. Manuel said he was, and I believed him. I

acted in good faith, and now you're tryin' to say I'm out my hard-earned money? I don't think so."

"Would you happen to know Mr. Manuel's current address?"

"No. He said he'd gotten an acting job in Los Angeles. That's why he needed to do everything in cash. I made him give me a receipt, though. And he said he'd contact me for the rent in a few months. That was fine with me. I'm paid up for a minute, anyway."

"This is a misunderstanding," Byron said, reading the lease, which looked legit. Manuel had made the agreement the day before the hearing, but Byron wasn't sure what took precedence. Manuel had been living in the house up until Judge Dunn's order, and as a resident, he had been able to make decisions regarding the property. Leasing it was another ball game, one where Byron didn't know the rules. The judge would have to get involved, and that made Byron edgy because the question became, where would Tia go in the interim?

Whether he was five miles away or three thousand, on the west coast, Manuel was doing a good job of sticking it to Tia.

"When did you meet with Manuel?" Byron asked Ms. Wilkes.

"Two weeks ago, Wednesday. I paid him forty-five hundred dollars, four months' rent in advance, and didn't have to pay a security deposit. So you tell crazy ass over there, this condo is legally mine. Here." She stomped into the foyer and pulled several boxes from against the wall and shoved them onto the porch with her foot.

"He said she might come for these." The woman

glared up at Byron. "I don't want to see her around here again. If I do, I'm gone kick ass first and take names later."

Pissed now that nothing had gone as planned, Byron pulled the handcuffs off his belt. "Are you threatening Ms. Amberson? If you are, I'll be glad to charge you and take you to jail."

"Brotha, please! If she ain't goin' to jail, I *definitely* ain't. Besides, I ain't threatenin' nobody. I'm *promising* that if she tries to break into *my* house again, she's going to meet Ms. Whoop Ass."

The door slammed in Byron's face, and he turned to look at Tia. Her eyes were round, and they widened as he walked down the stairs, his arms laden with her boxes. He could see her struggling to open the back door, but the futile attempt just further infuriated her.

He could hear her through the glass, screaming, "What the hell? What the hell? *What the hell*?"

He was asking himself the same damned thing. After arranging the boxes in the trunk, he opened the driver door and slid in.

"That's my house, and I want it back now."

"Tia, Manuel leased it, and the agreement looks legit. You're going to need a lawyer."

"Why?" she screeched. "I have you. You were told to get me into my house. You promised me this morning. I can't believe this. What the hell just happened?"

Byron turned around, bulletproof glass and metal separating him and Tia. Her face was taut from crying, her dark eyes piercing by the overhead light.

"He rented the place to her the day before the hearing," Byron said, striving to stay calm. "Manuel took forty-five hundred dollars from her, and now she refuses to leave."

"I'm the rightful owner of that condo. I'm supposed to be in there, not her! Do something!"

"Tia, first of all, quit screaming. Second, you snatched her damn near bald, *and* she has a legitimate lease agreement. You'll probably have to go through the process of evicting her."

"I'll take care of that right now. Let me out of this car. Evicting her isn't a problem for me. Come open this door. I'll do what you *couldn't* do."

Tia kept bumping the door with her shoulder, a slightly deranged look in her eyes.

Why were all women crazy?

"You're not going anywhere near that house. Tia," Byron said forcefully, trying to get her to look at him. She finally stopped moving. "I'll put in a few calls, and within the next couple days, we should have an answer as to how to get her out."

"Fine. Take me back to jail. At least there I had a room and a toilet. I think the ladies were getting used to my singing."

In his mind, Byron heard the toilet flushing on his career, not for the first time since he met Tia.

He felt something inside snap. Probably his sanity.

"You're not going back to jail. You're probably the only woman in the world that could commit ten felonies right now and get away with it. Damn!"

His outburst stunned her into silence, and he took advantage of her silence and rubbed his aching head.

Tia was right, but who the hell cared, because all the wrong things kept happening to her.

Byron calmly got out of the car and helped Tia

out of the backseat. He held her by the shoulders. "I'm going to look into this, and I'm going to get you an answer. I'm going to get you in your house, if I have to die trying. But you're going to have to trust me."

"Trust . . . you." She tried the words on for size, the crinkle around her nose expressing her inability to swallow them. "I would"—she raised her hand toward the closed condo door—"but my track record for trusting men is about as good as my ability to stay out of jail. I hope you understand."

She had a point.

"Where can I take you?" he asked.

"You're kidding, right?"

She shivered, and he realized how much colder the night had become. He assisted her into the car and turned on the heat.

It was pitch black outside, the neighbors snuggled inside their homes, having dinner. Tia should have been one of them, but here she was, again misplaced.

"Where's your car?" he asked. "I'll follow you and make sure you get settled in."

"Over there. Wait." Her voice rose slightly. "I don't see it in my space."

Tia looked around the parking lot, and Byron had a sinking feeling. He beat Tia out of the car and stabbed the air, indicating for her to stay in the vehicle. He took the stairs in threes and banged on the door.

Ida Wilkes took her sweet time answering the door before giving him the answers he needed. Pissed, he trotted down to the garbage can and retrieved a black garbage bag, threw it in the trunk, and climbed in the car.

Byron couldn't help himself and took pity on her. "Would you like me to get you some dinner before you go back to your friend's house?"

"Rachel and I kind of fell out."

Somehow, Byron wasn't shocked by this news. "Well, there's got to be someone else."

Tia looked down, folding her arms over her stomach.

"What's in the bag?" she asked.

"Your duvet. You told Dr. Khan you wanted it. You can have it dry-cleaned."

Her gaze rested on him so long, he grew uncomfortable.

There was so much behind her beautiful black lashes, and he wanted to know what she was thinking in the worst way. But he couldn't ask. Not after the day she'd had. "It's okay, Tia. It might not mean much, but I thought—"

"Thanks," she murmured. "Thank you."

Then she reached out and touched his hand and squeezed.

Byron did something he never did. He let it stay there.

"You're welcome. Any other family or friends you can stay with?"

"I've had a terrible run on friends lately." She cleared her throat and pulled her hand back. "It's ironic. We all got dumped on my birthday, Valentine's Day, and slowly but surely, we've all gone our separate, crazy ways."

Tia was abnormal again. She still didn't see any

of this as bizarre or even unusual, and the hard part was that he was starting to see things her way.

What did that mean? He was already attracted to her. Already had tasted the forbidden fruit and loved every microsecond of their kiss. Right now all he had to do was make a right onto I-285 and go home. He could have her in his bed in thirty minutes flat.

But then she'd be in his home. She'd be in his head. Her life would take on more significance than it already had, even though he spent a great deal of his day and night thinking and dreaming about her.

He'd saved her tonight from certain imprisonment, like he'd done for LaPrincess, but she was dead.

Byron thought hard on that, forcing himself to remember the feelings of betrayal and pain at knowing all his effort had gone to waste. Being a cop was hard. The people were memorable, but he didn't have to take them home and make love to them.

Thinking about making love to Tia was going to have to be enough.

Back on firm ground, Byron decided to get her where she had to go, and quickly. "Where are your folks?"

"Retired to Vegas. My father hated to disrupt his gambling by having to fly out there once a month. Now it's practically intravenous."

Again, Byron kept quiet. The more he got to know Tia, the more comical it became.

Tia was quiet too long. "What are you cooking up over there?" he asked.

"I'll have to go to Megan's. I'll ask her to let me stay a couple days. I don't have any other choice."

"That's a good temporary solution."

"What did she do to my car?"

"She had it towed."

Tia covered her face, and Byron braced for the tears. His sisters were always crying. He couldn't walk into his mother's house without somebody wailing about something. He was so used to it, he usually saw the tears and headed for the den to find his father. The old man was lucky, having going damn near deaf a couple of years ago. Whenever Byron's mother or his sisters started crying, his dad just turned up the TV real loud until nobody could stand being in the same room with him.

Byron looked at Tia just as she pulled her hands away from her face and folded them in her lap. No tears. Not a single drop. Now he really didn't know what to do. "Tia, I'll do my best to get your car back."

"Sure. Whatever."

"I will, Tia. I'm on your side."

"You already told me that."

They got under way, leaving the Lenox area behind.

Byron wondered how she'd make it over the next few weeks. Truthfully, it would probably take that long to get answers and a solution to the homeowner/rental mishap. He was almost sure she'd have to evict the tenant, but without being well-versed in property law, he couldn't think in exacts.

Byron shook his head. Dante Manuel was more than the illiterate idiot he'd presented himself as in court. His goal was to screw Tia over as badly as possible, and he was doing an amazing job.

They neared a fast-food restaurant, and Byron pulled into the drive-through. "Want a salad or something?"

She leaned close and studied the menu.

"Two number fives, super-sized. One with Coke, the other with hot coffee with three creams and four sugars. Six ketchups, please, and two salts."

He ordered, gazing at busy Buford Highway before looking at her. "You got a tapeworm or something?"

"Are you trying to stomp on my feelings? You offered and I'm eating. That a problem?"

Byron just threw up his hands.

Their food came, and she gave him directions to Megan's house. He drove down I-285, heading toward Chamblee, one of the most richly diversified areas of metro Atlanta. Traffic had petered off from rush hour but was thick enough to make them move slowly down Chamblee Tucker Road. In a way, he wished he'd waited to buy food over here, where the choices in cuisine were as varied as the residents.

But then again, Tia was contained, unable to wreak havoc on any of her unsuspecting neighbors.

"What's the penalty for assault and battery?" she asked, eating one french fry at a time, as if they were an expensive delicacy.

Byron choked on his and coughed, beating a yellow light. "Are you trying to get me fired? I gave you a break today with your boss. All I'm asking is for a few days to help you, and you want to know the penalty for A and B? Prison, dammit! Locked up for the longest possible sentence, if I have anything to do with it. Are we clear?"

She stared at him openmouthed. "No need to get hostile. Make a right, third building on the right," she snapped back.

Byron slammed on the brakes in front of the town house, got out, and started getting Tia's boxes out of the trunk. She finally made her way around back, her bags of food clutched to her chest.

"Put your coat on," Byron ordered, his breath fanning out in a cloud.

"I'm going inside in just a second."

"Tia," he growled, his head starting to hurt even more. "I went all the way back to work to get that coat. Put it on."

"Fine." She slid the coat on without further argument.

"Which place?" he asked.

"Up the stairs, the door on the left."

"Is she home?" Byron wondered. There appeared to be no movement inside.

"I guess. I told you she's recovering from her breakup and doing renovations."

"Good grief," he muttered, garnering a look from Tia.

"What's your problem?"

"You, your friends, and your luck. Scariest thing I've ever seen."

"Not our fault. We loved lousy men."

He knew that, but acknowledging it would make him feel sorry for her, as he'd done for LaPrincess, and then she'd go back to Manuel.

"Or," he said aloud, just to needle her, "you're all crazy. You've been driving me crazy since the day I met you."

She looked over her shoulder. "Tough." Tia rang the bell, waited, then laid into it.

"Don't you think that's being a little obnoxious?"

She didn't answer and, for five minutes straight,

punched the bell until it sounded like a screeching cat. Byron shifted the boxes and yanked her hand. "Come on. I know a women's shelter that'll take you for one night."

She folded her arms across her body, her posture saying she meant to have her way.

"I'm not going to a shelter! I'd go home with you before I'd go there. You wouldn't like that, would you?"

Byron was aware of all that he'd gone through for Tia. Even though this was his night off, and he was currently on his personal time, he was aware of every hellacious moment they'd spent together. But then he remembered when they'd been eye to eye, his body to hers, and he'd felt real wanting for her.

Even now, Tia was oblivious to his thoughts. Her going home with him was the just the beginning of what she could do for him.

Her gaze challenged him.

"You have no idea what I'd like, Tia. If I were you, I'd keep ringing that bell."

The depth of truth in his words caused her eyebrows to arch in that incredibly sexy way that was classically Tia. All he could think about was running his lips over hers and kissing every inch of her body.

If only he could put the boxes down and show her what was on his mind.

He could see her retreating by the twist to her mouth and the way she rolled her eyes. "I don't want to be the test dummy for your stun gun." Tia spun around and rapped on the door. "Megan! Open this door! I think she's coming," Tia said to Byron, although she didn't turn around again.

To his surprise, the inside lights flipped on, and

a woman snatched back the curtain. "Go away. I don't want company."

"Meg, I need a place to stay."

"Go to Rachel's. I can't have company right now."

"What are you? On a personal time-out? I need you," Tia yelled through the door.

"No."

The curtain fell back in place, and Bryon turned to go down the stairs. Tia . . . at his house . . . Everyone in hell was about to get a glass of ice water, apparently.

Tia smacked the door with her palm. "Megan Patricia Lewis, I've been your best friend since college. I've nursed you through the breakup of forty-six boyfriends, your two-day lesbian phase, and your religious conversions, all six of them! I loaned you money for having that mole removed from your nipple and for your Brazilian wax, which you didn't even tell me about, or else I wouldn't have been caught by surprise by Mr. 'cut it all off!' Now if you can't do me this one favor, the one and only time that I've ever asked you for anything, then you're just a lousy, selfish, crazy piece of crap for a friend!"

Byron just shook his head and tried not to absorb the insanity. He also vowed to go to church on Sunday.

They didn't hear a sound from inside.

Fed up, he pounded the door with his fist.

"Hey! Tia was in jail all last night," Byron barked. "And if you don't let her stay here, I'm going to take her back to jail and lock her up."

The curtain didn't move as Tia stood at the door, shivering.

Byron lowered the boxes to get his handcuffs.

He wasn't taking any chances. "Come on. We're going back."

"She's my friend," Tia replied confidently, trying to see through the curtained glass. "Just give her a minute."

Byron counted to sixty. Obviously, not that good a friend. He reached for Tia's delicate wrist.

The door creaked open. "Is that true?"

Tia launched herself inside the door. "Yes. It's just for a couple days. Bless you, Megan."

Tia flipped on lights as she walked inside, Megan trailing, dousing them. Byron retrieved the boxes and unloaded them inside the foyer, went back for the duvet, and stopped inside the living room. He stared at the walls and wondered if this was his worst nightmare come true. Tia flipped on the overhead living room light.

The pictures on the wall confirmed it. This was the tenth floor of hell.

"Oh! Crap!" Tia exclaimed, and dropped her bags of dinner, as she stared at the life-size drawing of a man on the wall, his private parts obliterated by the real hammer still wedged into the drywall. Pink insulation poked out of the crotch area, tufts on the floor.

Megan used the heel of her hand to massage her temple. "I haven't been myself lately."

Byron eased his hand up toward his gun as he looked at all the depictions of the woman's former lover. In each one, he was castrated in some form or another.

"Want some water?" Megan offered, shuffling off to the kitchen without waiting for their answer.

"Feels like I'm in a horror museum," Tia whispered to Byron as she took off her coat.

For once they were on the same side.

"I didn't know they had museums for the criminally insane."

"She's just venting. A lot. This is hardly criminal. A few drawings."

"Fourteen. Definitely insane."

"Here's your water." Megan handed them drinking glasses full of red and brown paint. "I think I'm thirsty." She shuffled off again, went into the bathroom, and closed the door.

Byron shook his head, his gaze never leaving Tia's.

"Thanks for the ride," she told him, now that the level of insanity in the room had dimmed.

He laughed. Spontaneous and hard. "You're kidding, right? You can't stay here. She gave us paint for water and went to the bathroom to get herself a drink. She's a total whack job."

Tia looked around like she understood the madness. "That is a little off, but, whatever. Think of it this way. She's not hurting anyone. And she didn't say anything about hearing voices. I'm staying. I'll be fine here."

Byron allowed Tia to put her hand on his back and walk him to the front door. She took his cup of paint and set it in the corner on the floor.

"Admit that she's crazy, and I might let you stay."

Her mouth turned down in a smirk. "Megan is going to be fine. I can handle her."

"Why would I believe that? *You* can't handle *you*. You still have Ms. Wilkes's dandruff under your fingernails."

Tia's lips folded into her mouth, and before he knew it, they were chuckling. She smiled, and it reminded him of the dawning of a new day. Despite everything they'd been through, he wanted to kiss her again. To pull her against him, wrap her in his arms, and taste her breath. Hadn't she mentioned something about a Brazilian wax? He wouldn't be able to get that off his mind, even if he had a rocket launcher.

Tia leaned into him, and he touched her arms to hold her off, but his hands defied his brain and let her come closer, until their mouths hovered a whisper apart. Time slipped.

Then he saw the tip of her tongue. The last cord of resistance dissolved, and he let his tongue greet hers. All the feelings he'd suppressed beneath duty and responsibility roared to the surface, and he let lust and desire flow through his body.

They were finally on the same page, in an alignment he understood. He really wanted to take her home. Byron lifted her closer to him, pressing the air from between them. Dressed, he couldn't get any closer.

"Excuse me," Megan said, blasting light on them.

Byron's eyes struggled to assimilate to his surroundings. He bolted away from Tia, sanity rushing to his brain while all his stored sexual energy pooled between his legs.

"What are you looking for?" Tia asked Megan, rubbing her hands over her mussed hair. Her lips looked so delicious. Byron had to look away before he made a fool of himself.

Megan looked confused. "I forgot. Good night." She went to her bedroom, closed the door, and burst out crying. Her heartbreaking sobs had the same effect as if she'd tossed ice on a candle.

Tia looked up at Byron, a thousand words rushing to her eyes even before she opened her mouth.

He braced himself for rejection, although he knew he should have been the one to go there first.

"I don't regret that kiss," Tia said, "so, don't think I'm going to take it back."

How had she known he was going to say they should have been smarter and not let their emotions get the best of them?

Logic dictated he be reasonable, except his penis was like a lightning rod for her. If he took back everything, he'd sound like Fred. And Byron was no punk.

Besides, regret wasn't anywhere close to how he was feeling. "I'm not taking it back." He caressed her jaw, wishing he had more time to explore her. But she and her friend were fragile. Too fragile. In the light of day, this would look differently. "In fact, that's the last thing on my mind."

"Good."

"Promise me you're not going to leave here," Byron said, trying to create some emotional distance, or else he wouldn't leave Tia, tonight or any time soon.

"Promise."

"You two aren't going on a secret mission of seek and destroy?"

"That's ridiculous. I don't even know where Dante is."

Byron was impressed and went three for three. "Promise you're going to forget the past and look ahead."

She shrugged tentatively. "Promise, with a caveat."

He was on the porch as she stood in the doorway. Cold air brushed past him and scattered goose bumps across her arms, but she didn't seem to notice. "He tried to destroy me. Break me down, humiliate me, and strip me of my self-esteem and all that I've worked for. I have to get him. It's the principle. One good time—don't worry, nothing fatal—then I'll move on. Thanks for everything, Officer Rivers. I'm sure I'll be seeing you soon. Good night."

For the second time that night, a door closed in his face, and Byron stood there, knowing the other shoe he'd been waiting to drop was firmly wedged up his butt.

Chapter Sixteen

All of Tia's senses sprang to life as her eyes peeled
open to off-key singing, the thin odor of oil-based
paint and pancakes. Her gut did a bump and roll,
peeved at the combination of stomach acid and the
two bottles of Pinot Grigio she and Megan had con-
sumed last night.

Right now she just felt like the empty bottle that
gaped at her from the floor. Sapped of its useful-
ness and discarded.

She blotted out Megan's singing, turning on the
air mattress, when her hip hit wood. It seemed the
bed had deflated some during the night. Pity shot
through her nose to her eyes, making them water.

Not only was she single and homeless, but she
had a big butt, too. A dry sob tore from her throat,
and a putrid cloud of bad breath filled the air
around her face.

Tia scrunched up her nose.

What had her life come to? What had she done
wrong in a past life to deserve this?

She pushed to her hands and knees, her ears

ringing. She eyed her swinging boobs beneath her pajama top and wondered if she and the girls would ever be happy again.

When *was* the last time she'd been happy?

Things with Dante hadn't been great for a long time, Tia admitted to herself. She'd been holding out, hoping they'd return to the way they'd been accustomed to. To their various friends and associates, their relationship had been the one others aspired to achieve.

They'd been the young, urban professionals, driving cute, fast cars, club-hopping through Midtown, with their place close enough to Atlanta that all they had to do was look out the window and gaze at the skyline, with the dawning sun.

They'd had it all. It seemed.

But Tia knew of the scars and the breaks in the double-paned glass of their false life. Yet she'd stayed, hoping things would get better. Waiting for her life to mirror the fairy tale she'd created.

The truth was, she'd wanted it to work. She didn't believe in abandoning relationships.

She'd learned that from her mother. Her father gambled like he had the money of a sheik, but had Millicent Amberson left him? No. Every night, as her father slept, her mother did everything short of an exorcism, all to no avail. Lately, she'd joined the "if you can't beat 'em" school of thought.

Tia recognized that road as the one she'd lived on for over a year. She'd tried to wait out Dante's run of bad luck and irresponsibility and to be there when he turned back into the man she'd fallen in love with.

She pushed off her hands and stood, wrapping

herself in an old summer dress, which would have
to make do as a robe. This was her road now. This
dead-end street. Humiliation seized her throat,
anger drying the stale saliva on her tongue. She
had to retaliate, if Dante ever turned up. On principle. Just as she'd told Byron last night.

Thinking of their kiss, she peered out the
window, expecting to see his squad car, but the lot
was full of civilian vehicles waiting to be driven to
work. She thought of her towed car but didn't have
the energy to get angry. The truth was she couldn't
afford gas or parking right now, so taking the bus
was the cheaper option.

Tia wouldn't go so far as to thank ugly Ida Wilkes,
but she had eliminated one decision for Tia to
make every day. Now Tia would add that gas and
parking money to the pot she was saving for an attorney.

She searched for Byron's car again but was disappointed.

She was just feeling sorry for herself, and maybe
the sad woman inside of her sought his attention
because it was better than none at all. Tia understood these feelings. She knew she'd get stronger,
and that eventually, Byron would be part of her
past, as Dante was.

Instead of her mood improving, her heart sank a
little further. Tia watched as a lady scampered down
the stairs of her town home and raced for the bus
stop. The bus pulled away, reminding Tia that she
needed to get ready for work.

Energized, she hurried into the living room for
her bags and stopped short.

Megan was on the six-foot-high scaffolding,

completing the *k* after f-u-c in lime green. She'd already drawn ugly depictions of Sonny below, while singing a bad rendition of Kelly Price's "Heartbreak Hotel." "Now I see that you've been doin' wrong, played me all along. . . ."

"Hey," Tia said tentatively.

"Hey. And made a fool of me," Megan sang, staring at Tia, then slopping the brush onto the wall.

Tia covered her hair with a sheet of newspaper. "Um, Sweetie, the workmen are coming in this morning. You're not really helping them."

"I know." Megan stabbed a period after the *k*.

"Just working out a little aggression?"

"Yep. Just a little," Megan said in a tiny voice. "You did some nice work in the other room."

Tia's rank mouth soured a bit more. She passed her bag on the floor, went into the living room, and couldn't contain her laughter. "We're crazy," she exclaimed.

She'd drawn a picture of the last time she'd seen Dante. Bad Jheri curl, too small suit, a five o'clock shadow that was just nasty, and yellow teeth. He looked like Shenaynay on crack.

Shaking her head, Tia grabbed her bag. "I hope they tear this wall down first."

"They are. That's why I painted it. The evidence will be gone by next Friday."

Megan had gotten down, and Tia patted her shoulder. "I'm glad to hear your voice returning to normal. I've got to get to work before I have no job to go back to."

"Want me to call in a bomb scare? That'll buy you some time."

Tia blinked, a little scared. "Dang, Megan, step

away from the detonator switch. People aren't fond of desperate women doing stupid things if they're not a size two and on TV. You'd better get ready for work, too. Aren't you on days now?"

"I got put on leave."

Megan walked into the other room, humming the chorus.

"When did that happen?"

"The day after I was at the airport. Apparently, Clayton County is concerned I might not be stable. Want me to pick up some male voodoo dolls later? We can drink wine, play with the Ouija board, and have fun."

The phone book balanced the lamp from the living room. Tia sat on the floor and leafed through it.

"Sorry. No time for witchcraft, but you can call my cousin Leroy. I've got to get an attorney to get my house back."

"It's a woman, right?" Megan said. "I can scare her out of there. Women are wimps."

While Tia entertained the thought, the last image of Ms. Wilkes holding her hair in her hand, a murderous look on her face, had convinced Tia to stay with her current plan. "Thanks, Sweetie, but I need to do this legally."

". . . Heartbreak Hotel," Megan sang. "Let me know if you change your mind."

Tia glanced at the clock and scribbled several names of attorneys on the back of her Macy's bill. Grimacing at where she knew the balance hovered, she made a good list and put the phone book back under the lamp.

Dialing one that promised twenty-four-hour

service, she waited. "Cavitt and Savage. This is Rusty Cavitt."

Tia's eyebrow itched. The man sounded like he'd sucked on one too many nails.

"Hello. What is your retainer fee?" she asked.

"What's the problem?"

"I was granted my condo in a legal settlement against my boyfriend, who I lived with, but before the court date, he rented the condo. I own it. Judge Dunn granted it to me."

"So how'd he rent it?"

Tia sighed, not wanting to relive the whole thing. "Before we got the order from the judge, he was living there and rented it. Then I got into a fight with Ms. Wilkes, the tenant, and the police were there . . . It's complicated. I just need to know how much you cost."

Rusty snorted. "I'm only guessing where this will go, so conservatively, seventy-five hundred dollars."

"You're kidding."

"Now you listen up," he said real friendly. "There's two things I never joke about. God and money."

"Do you take a payment—"

"Little sister, before you go on, let me tell you somethin'. I do my business like in the old days. Cash on the barrel. If you want me as your legal counsel, I cost seventy-five hundred dollars. If you don't have that retainer, we can part friends now and hang up."

"Thank you," she said belatedly and took his advice.

Two additional calls resulted in chuckles, accompanied by the same fee or higher. Discouraged, Tia opened the phone book and got more names, staying away from the attorneys with ads. She flipped back a few pages, hoping the farther back in the book, the cheaper.

Her logic wasn't fail-safe, and she could feel her heart sinking with every no.

Finally, she got up, kicking aside the fast-food containers from last night, and dragged her bag with her.

"Meg, I'm going to shower. Are you sure you don't want to stop that and maybe talk to somebody?"

A fist-sized circle emerged as Megan stroked white paint over Sonny's crotch in the latest depiction of him. "That's a little like the pot calling the kettle black, isn't it? If you want to stay here, don't judge me, and I won't throw you out. Agreed?"

Megan never once turned from her painting, but the low-grade undercurrent of anger resonated all the way to the bathroom. "Okay," Tia said.

"When you get home, we can finish the one of Dante. Maybe add fire to his hair. It *is* combustible. Wouldn't that be fun to see in person?"

A gurgle erupted in Tia's throat. "Yeah. No, definitely not."

Would the three-day hold down at Grady's mental hospital apply here? "I have to think about a part-time job. The attorney is going to be expensive," Tia added.

Megan made gray tears on Sonny's face, with a thin brush, then neatened them with her pinky finger. Tia watched her facial features and how they softened as she caressed the paint into position. She still loved him. Enough to hate him.

"Part-time job? You can hardly keep up with the

job you have now. Sell those purses. You have so many, you won't miss a few."

Tia regarded the beloved box of bags that sat discarded in the crowded hallway. Had there been enough room in her temporary bedroom, in the midst of Megan's forgotten drum set, the AB Scissor, and the sewing machine, Tia would have slept with her purses. Besides losing the man she'd been committed to, she'd lost her lifestyle. With nothing to hold on to but the bags as reminders of better days, Tia felt a lonely panic climb her body.

"I can't," she said, knowing the whisper in her voice magnified her weakness.

She needed Kate Spade, Louis Vuitton, Prada, and her coveted Charles David, which she bought off a wild-eyed woman last New Year's Eve at the Hilton for fifty dollars. Her bags were handpicked. And worth thousands.

Tia stroked the handle of her Marc Jacobs, then settled on the Baby Phat green vinyl tote, pushing through the box for her Gucci and Coach bags.

"I can't sell them. Hey, they're not all here."

"She must have kept some. Probably didn't know the ones she kept weren't the most valuable. People sure are stupid."

Anger flamed in Tia's stomach as weariness surrounded her. "I'm so tired of fighting for everything."

"You can't give up. We can just go over there and get them back."

"I can't right now. I have to focus on getting my place back. Besides, Byron wasn't kidding about taking me back to jail." Tia unwrapped two Tums and chewed. "Jail just isn't my thing. I'm going to shower, then get out of here."

"Suit yourself." Megan started singing "Heart-break Hotel" in an off-key soprano.

Tia hurried into the bathroom, taking two additional bags with her. *Sell them?*

Megan was high on paint fumes.

Resolve strengthened Tia. She'd find another job today. If she just opened up her mind and put good thoughts into the universe, good things would happen. She did a modified meditation as she hopped into the shower.

When she was finally dressed and headed out the door, she could feel the good vibes all the way to the bus stop.

Her head high, Tia knew her life was about to change. Not even the sight of Byron's patrol car trailing the bus to her job could dampen her spirits.

Chapter Seventeen

"Tia, can I see you outside, please?"

The photos of purses in Tia's hands confirmed Byron's suspicions, but he didn't want to jump to any conclusions. He'd done that before, with disastrous consequences.

Today's break-in at her condo could be a coincidence. The only thing was that he didn't believe in coincidences and neither did his captain.

Byron believed that happenstance incidents were the mechanics of women, orchestrated to trick men into doing what they wanted. He'd heard it numerous times from his cop buddies.

"Yo, I met her in the meat section of the grocery store. She was just standing there, and I helped her pick out beef tips. How'd she know those were my favorites? It's like she knew everything about me."

It wasn't until later that his friend found out that his new woman and the cashier were cousins, and they'd scoped out his shopping habits and had set a trap.

Now, one year after they first met, his friend had

two jobs to support baby twins, her son from a prior relationship, an SUV, a minivan—which he drove—and an expensive house in Cascade, which they couldn't afford. The wife couldn't work and help with the bills. She had postpartum depression and had to get two massages a week—so he was pulling the whole load.

Byron shrugged. No way was a woman sticking it to him like that. He wasn't a fool.

Byron believed what his eyes could see, and the evidence was in Tia's pretty little hands.

She stopped outside the room. "What's on your mind?"

"What have you got there?"

Her eyes darted from side to side, as if she didn't know what he was talking about. "Nothing?" she said sarcastically.

"May I?" Byron slid the pictures from her hands. "Nice," he murmured, counting thirteen in all. Just the number of purses Ms. Wilkes had reported stolen while she'd been at work today.

"What are you planning to do with these?" Byron asked.

"You interested in carrying a purse? Might be a little over the top for the down low, but, hey, to each his own. Ronnie/Rhonda will be glad. You might free your mind and rid yourself of all your stress up in here." She made a sweeping gesture from his head to his feet.

He took her insult in stride. "I'm a straight man, sweetheart. You know that for a fact, so you're not going to distract me. I got a call from the precinct. Somebody broke into Ms. Wilkes's place and relieved her of about thirteen purses, but left all the credit cards and other valuables alone."

"First of all"—Tia snatched the photos from him—"she has valuables? I doubt that. Second, the condo is mine. Third, I can't steal my own stuff."

"Ms. Wilkes seems to think so."

Byron stared at her furious eyes, and he wanted her like crazy. One day wanting her would get him into trouble. He felt that inside. But Byron couldn't help himself.

"Why would I steal my own purses, then take pictures of them? That's just idiotic for anyone to even think that."

"Are you calling *me* an idiot?"

She didn't open her mouth, but her look said, What do you think?

"What?" he demanded.

"You're a terrible detective."

"Hey!"

"Hey, hell." The smooth column of her neck worked, swallowing what he assumed was a profanity. "I know you don't think much of me, but I'm selling my purses on the Internet so I can raise money to get an attorney so I can get my house back. I'm already registered on eBay. And, *Mr. Police Detective*, these are the same bags you brought into the house last night. Satisfied?"

Byron glanced at the photos again. He had carried boxes, and there had been purses, but he hadn't bothered to inspect the contents of each box. *Damn.* She had him again.

He stood in the hallway, where he'd been made a fool of too many times to count, and old resentment shot through him.

He should have done better detective work before coming to her. She was stressed out, and she had a right to be.

There was one thing about Tia, and that was she was definitely transparent. She didn't bother to try to deceive him or anyone. And, on the other hand, Ms. Wilkes had everything to lose.

Why hadn't he thought of all this before approaching Tia? Because he wanted to categorize her, and as he was learning, Tia Amberson didn't fit the mold. "I can't hold you," he conceded.

"Brilliant deduction," she said, deceptively calm. "Now if you'll excuse me, I really need anger management class tonight." Her voice dropped. "All day I've been wanting to get something long, thick, and soft or hard in the palm of my hand and then snap it in half!" She exhaled sharply. "Ever get that urge, Officer?"

She was definitely turning the crazy corner like her friend. "That's Detective, and I have a lot of other uses for my hands, soft or hard, notwithstanding." Byron matched her even tone, then checked himself, the innuendo guiding them where he'd been wanting to take her for some time. "I will check on your story."

"You do that, Mr. Efficient. You should worry about what I don't tell you."

Byron gazed down at her but didn't respond. She always seemed to have the upper hand.

Tia started to go through the door, but he blocked her just in time, as Pebbles steamrolled in, dragging Ginger with her.

"Do you see her face? Why is she here *and* still

getting her butt kicked by her fool husband?" Pebbles shouted to the classroom full of students.

Byron followed Tia inside and tried to control an instinctive wince. Ginger's face had taken the brunt of her ex's rage, finger marks imprinted on her cheeks, her lip split and swollen. He'd seen domestic abuse before, and it was never something he got used to.

The women in the class crowded around Ginger in a protective circle.

Tia shook him free, moving into the center.

Ginger smiled bravely. "Ladies, I'm fine."

"You're fine, with your eye swollen shut?" Pebbles demanded, angry tears spilling down her cheeks. "This doesn't make sense."

"Why did this happen?" Debbie wanted to know.

"He wants me to stay married to him. He wants to use my money for his lifestyle. I'd hired some people who were able to get back the money he initially took. So he came home Monday and begged me to forgive him." Her head dipped. "I did, thinking he had changed. He's not even converting to a different faith. He just wants me to participate in that lifestyle with him in Utah."

"In bigamy?"

"No. Polygamy." Ginger's soft voice hitched. "I just can't. I want him. Not a life he shares with other women."

"You said no, and he did this to you?" Peggy asked, hovering over Ginger.

"I called the police, and they came out and took a report. These officers have been to the house several times. I think they're tired of me."

Grumbles livened up the crowd.

"The police don't care about us. That's why we're in this class instead of our spouses," Debbie insinuated.

"They have other, more serious, things to worry about," Pebbles stressed. "Domestic abuse just isn't a priority."

"Yes, it is," Byron asserted. "There are officers dedicated to domestic cases. They're a high priority for all police departments."

"We need to stop depending on the law to fix our problems and deal with our lying, no-good, two-timing, low-life, lazy men ourselves. Every one of them deserves to have his butt handed to him!" Pebbles shouted.

"Yeah!" a chorus of women cheered Pebbles's irrational tirade.

"Ladies, please," Fred pleaded. "Let's start by writing in our journals. Instead of letting this passionate moment slip away, we can examine our levels of anger and work through them constructively. We are at the point where we can state our affirmations and walk away from troubling situations."

Ten disbelieving glares were shot at Fred, who backed into the blackboard and bumped his head.

"I didn't do anything to provoke him," Ginger said, pleading her case. "I took him back. That's what he asked. If I go back home, he's going to hurt me. I can't live that way."

"Don't go home, Ginger," Lacy stated.

"Make the police do their jobs," Ann Marie advised. "Make them uphold the law."

"Or we can do it ourselves to each and every one of them." Pebbles struggled to her feet.

Byron held up his hands, stepping in front of the unsettled group. "Ladies, I'm an officer with the Atlanta

Police Department." Angry grumbles resounded. "Revenge isn't the answer. If you seek vengeance against him or anybody, you'll be prosecuted, and you'll go to jail. I'm telling you, it's not worth it. Let the courts mete out justice."

"You're a spy!" Ann Marie screamed. "I'll bet you were sent here by one of our husbands."

All of the woman glared at him. "Who sent you? Was it my husband, Brent? Is he trying to get ammunition for a divorce?" Peggy demanded.

"I was my husband's affair before he divorced his wife and married me. Now I guess he's got something new, and he wants me gone. Is that it?" Ann Marie said.

"Ladies, I'm not a spy. I was sent here as a punishment, which is why we're all here," Bryon reminded them. "Retaliation isn't the answer. You'll just end up in a worse situation. Let us do our jobs."

"You're not doing your job good enough. Her face is evidence of that," Lacy said matter-of-factly.

"Fred, we're taking a break," Debbie told him.

"We're just about to begin," Fred told them.

"You want us to journal first?" Pebbles grabbed her notebook, and the other women followed suit.

"Yes," Fred said, his face hopeful that the worst was over. "We're going to come up with reasonable solutions on how to use our anger constructively."

"Okay. I think I'll get a drink and write in my journal in the commons area," Tia said, and started out.

The other women grabbed their books and purses as a chorus of "me toos" rang out.

"Oh-oh." Fred stuttered, unable to think fast enough to stop them from leaving. "Okay. Take a break and come back . . ."

He gave up. No one was listening.

After the door closed with a decisive snap, Byron turned on Fred. "Was that the best you could do?"

"You weren't so great yourself. They think you're a husband spy," Fred shot back hotly, shocking Byron. The man had finally asserted himself.

Fred folded the short sleeves up and down on his shirt. "What do you think they're going to do when they come back? Beat me up? I can't handle another woman hitting me."

The tiny balloon of respect Byron had developed for Fred exploded. "You're abused, too?"

"When I was fourteen. In PE. We were playing touch football. A girl I liked tackled me. That really hurt. I haven't forgotten."

"Man, you're pathetic."

"At least I know when I'm in over my head. You're the law," Fred said, uncharacteristically belligerent. "Do you think they're cooking up a plan?"

"I'm almost certain of it."

Alarm made Fred wipe his comb-over repeatedly. "What do you think they'll do?"

Byron sighed in resignation. "Follow the tradition of scorned women."

Fred walked to the desk, put on his Mr. Rogers sweater, and began packing his things.

"What are you doing?" Byron wanted to know.

"Firing myself. It's inevitable. I'm no good at this. You already knew that. I'm trying to think of a new occupation for myself that doesn't involve dealing with people. Maybe there's a job in forestry."

"Do you know anything about dendrology, the study of trees?"

"No," Fred admitted. "But there's no people. That's a bonus."

Byron took Fred's backpack, put his colored pens and notebook back on the desk, and shoved the book *How to Deal With Strong-Willed Women* deep into the canvas. If the women saw that, they'd have poor Fred in a bra and panties before eight-thirty.

"Fred, you're staying."

"Help me, Jesus," Fred whispered and put his head down on his desk. His comb-over flapped onto his arm, and he didn't even bother to fix it.

Neatness and order had always been a part of Byron's life, but even he wasn't going to touch another man's hair.

"You're going to have to take control. Reiterate why we're here," Byron told the defeated man.

"And what are you going to do? Arrest them all for choosing bad men? Leave me alone, if you don't mind. I feel sorry for you."

"Why?"

"You still hope. I have a friend who drives for M.A.R.T.A. Maybe he can hit me with his bus. We can make it look like I fell. I fall all the time. That won't be hard."

"Shut up, Fred. You wouldn't die."

A short sob jumped out of Fred's mouth as his head hit his chest. "Just my miserable luck." He whimpered into the fold of his arm, sounding like a sick dog.

Byron stared at the bald spot on his teacher's head, aggravated that the man didn't have more testosterone.

Well, it didn't matter. He was an officer of the law, and his job was to serve and protect. Everyone.

Even dumb ass, abusive husbands married to these very angry women.

The women were just blowing off steam, he told himself.

The anger management course was ending soon, and they wouldn't jeopardize completion of this class for short-term satisfaction.

There was one thing he could do.

While Fred regrouped, Byron took the list of names, addresses, and e-mail addresses to the office down the hall and copied them, before slipping them back into Fred's bag.

Outside again, he dialed the precinct and relayed the information to the duty sergeant and requested that a patrol car be sent over to pick up Ginger's husband. Perhaps with him being gone when she got home, that would allay any further thoughts of retribution.

He snapped his phone shut just as Tia and the rest of the class entered and took their seats.

They were calm. Collected. Quiet. Something was wrong. The anger was gone. In its place was eerie, cold, calculated resolve, which no man ever wanted to see on the face of one woman, let alone nine of them.

Fred raised his head in time to see the women's silent procession and tried to crawl under his desk. When he couldn't get under, he was left hyperventilating in his chair.

Byron gestured to Tia to meet him outside the room, and she rose.

The women looked at her with warning glares, but she reassured them by waving her hand, and they backed down.

What the hell was going on?

"What is it?" she asked, leaving the door half open.

Her perfume made him want to kiss her neck and do things he'd only imagined to her body. "What are you planning?" he asked, focusing.

"None of your business."

"You're going to poison them? They're all going to have some mysterious accidents, right? You do remember what jail was like, right? Want to go back as perpetrator, accessory before and after the fact?" He got really close to her. "Do you want Manuel to take everything from you, including your freedom?"

"I'm over him. I just want my home back."

Tia's words temporarily paralyzed him. Byron wasn't sure whether to be angry or afraid that he hadn't nipped this in the bud a long time ago. He crossed his arms, not believing her.

The Tia he knew wanted to skin Manuel and hang his rotting flesh outside the lingerie department at Macy's as the national symbol for all angry women.

"That's quite an about-face."

"I'm told that's a woman's prerogative."

A humorless chuckle shook him. "Not unless she has something comparable to replace it with. You've wanted revenge far too long, far too deeply. That desire wouldn't just fly away, Tia."

"I'd think you'd be happy to not have to follow me around anymore. Excuse me. I have a class to finish."

As she passed, Byron caught the scent of strawberry shampoo. It clouded his judgment, and he had to fight the urge to hold her still and do naughty things to her.

She passed him, and when she looked back, he

saw deceit in her eyes. The lightbulb in his brain went off. He snagged her arm, and electricity shot to the soles of his feet.

"You're not fooling me. You're all going after Ginger's husband."

"Why would you think that?"

He held her gaze for as long as possible. She was up to no good, and that frustrated him. Up until now, he could almost understand Tia's desire to get back at Manuel. But revenge on a man for another woman? That was just stupid.

And that wasn't Tia. "You're a fool if you do this. I'm a cop. I have to do my job. You're going to screw up, and I won't be able to help you."

"Like you have in the past?"

"That's right," Byron assured her.

She tilted her head to the side. "Thank you for helping me stab myself, get thrown in jail. And most of all, thank you for helping me get back into my home. Knowing you has been priceless."

Ouch. "Don't do this, Tia."

There was no question Tia had been dealt a bad hand, but a better future was on the horizon. If Tia didn't deviate, she'd have everything she deserved.

But what if she liked her walk on the wild side of life?

What if this was the new Tia forever?

"Byron, Tia, will you two please take your seats?" Fred called toward the door, sounding weary.

"Just a minute," Byron replied, turning back to Tia, whom he hadn't released. "Am I right? Are you all planning to kill Ginger's husband?"

"No."

"What are you going to do to him?"

She squirmed. "I have nothing to say to you."

"Dammit, Tia."

Byron tried to make her look at him, but she wouldn't.

"I've taken an oath of secrecy, Byron, so don't try to get information from me."

"You're a grown woman, but you're playing a petty, childish game."

She yanked her arm away but stepped back to face him. "All you men are alike. When you don't get what you want, you try to bully us. When that doesn't work, you threaten and blackmail. And when that doesn't work, some men beat on their women. What exactly are we supposed to do? Keep trusting that eventually your word is going to be good enough? I'm sick to death of hearing your promises. The rest of the women are, too."

"I told you the police—"

"Can't do a damned thing. I'm not in my house, and you're the police! Ginger's face carries the rage of her husband, and you're arguing with me about what you think might happen to him, a spousal abuser." She shook her head. "I'm not telling you anything. If you want to know what's going on in my life or what we're planning, I guess you can keep doing what you've been doing."

"And what's that?"

"Watching my ass."

Tia snatched the door open and walked into the classroom, leaving him standing alone.

He watched her all right, and when the door closed, he punched his fist into his palm, wishing he could take her and her smart mouth and make love to her until every bit of her was so satiated she didn't want to do anything but sleep.

He hated it again, but Tia was right.

Law enforcement had let them down. He'd definitely disappointed Tia, and there was no excuse for what happened to Ginger.

The women had a right to be angry. And they were going to exercise that right. Foreboding was a luxury feeling, an emotion most men didn't ever experience. But he'd grown up with four sisters and a mother. He knew when bad news was heading his way.

This was a Category 5 hurricane. And if he wanted to keep his job, he'd have to conquer this storm on his own.

He was already in Tia's life. He had to now make himself at home there and convince her and the rest of the women to let their anger go.

In his gut, he knew someone's life depended upon it.

Chapter Eighteen

Tia dropped the newly edited copy into the bin for the evening weatherman, Ben Macklin, and walked back to her cube.

It was nearly seven-thirty p.m., and once again, Chance had pulled the trick move and let the interns go home without the editing for the late show being completed. As the senior flunky, Tia knew if the work wasn't done, Ben would pitch a fit. Then his producer, Barb, would complain to Chance, and somehow it would be Tia's fault. She was just trying to head trouble off at the pass.

The truth was she didn't mind staying. With no home of her own to go to, she wasn't in a rush to embrace Megan's madness too soon.

Back at her cube, she absorbed the quiet, letting it sink into her restless body. Her ankle popped, and she stretched the other one just enough to elicit an echoing response. How her mother hated that she and her father cracked their bones, as she called it.

I'm getting old. She'd just celebrated a birthday,

and the highlight of her day was a comparison of how she and her father made noises with their bodies.

Nostalgia and homesickness wrapped her in the scent of freesia from her mother's large bosom and Polo from her daddy's bear hugs.

She wanted them to be on Beverly Crossing Way in Stone Mountain, Georgia, the way they'd been for twenty-nine years. Then she could have gone home when all this trouble had started with Dante, and she could have lain in her queen-size bed and looked at the stars she'd stenciled on her ceiling during freshman year in high school and fixed her jacked-up life.

She wouldn't have slashed the tires or stabbed herself in the foot, and she wouldn't be in trouble at work. She'd have money and her purses, and she'd have a nice home. And she wouldn't have an overwhelming desire to be in her childhood bedroom, fantasizing about a new life.

Opening her desk, Tia looked closely at the drawer, expecting to see her change.

Sifting through her papers, she searched for the money, then shrugged. Maybe one of the guys had borrowed it and would give it back tomorrow. Most of them didn't know how cash-strapped she was, and she wasn't going to tell them that her finances had more holes than a fisherman's net. She needed her change for dinner.

Disappointed, Tia clicked the computer mouse and went to the online site where she'd listed her purses. Two had sold! Champagne bubbles of elation sparkled through her. Five hundred dollars was now in her account. She'd package the purses as soon as she got home and get them in the mail tomorrow.

From her direct deposit paycheck, she quickly paid her mortgage and other bills, leaving herself with just over fifty dollars in spending money until her next check, in two weeks. A message popped up reminding her to mail her taxes, and Tia groaned. She still had yet to compile them, but she was probably going to get a refund. Making a note on a piece of paper, Tia shoved it in her bag. She'd get on that tonight.

First, though, she'd have to stop by the ATM and get money out to last the rest of the month. Maybe more bags would sell soon. If several of the more expensive bags sold, she'd have enough to get an attorney and get her home back. Then her life would be on track.

In the meantime, she dialed the judge's clerk and left a message to get on his calendar. Tia had no idea how this was done, but it looked as if Judge Dunn's prediction would come true. She rationalized, if she got on his calendar, she could always get an attorney faster.

Seeing three e-mails from her anger management classmates, Tia opened the first one.

Revenge plan one: We should pull a Stella and burn his clothes and all his possessions. See how he likes playing Mr. Man in clothes from the thrift store.

Tia giggled, knowing the author was Pebbles.

Been there, seen that. We need to be much more original. Gary should suffer. We should give him a little something to help him sleep, cut all the hair off his body and tattoo INFIDEL across his forehead. I know a guy who'll give us a discount. Love, Debbie.

Tia's laughter echoed in the stillness of the quiet office.

The idea was original, but it wasn't without flaws. Michael Jordan had made bald fine back in the nineties. Once Gary got over being bald, his hair would grow back, covering their work, and even then, some women would still feel sorry for him.

Tia clicked on the next e-mail.

Take away what he wants most.

She looked to identify the sender but didn't recognize the address. The tone of the message creeped her out.

Several of the ladies responded, asking for more details, but others weighed in on the first two suggestions.

Tia voted for tattooing but added that it should be little *I*'s all over his face, with slow-fading ink. The whole idea smacked of the seventeenth century and *The Scarlet Letter*.

An old punishment for an old crime.

Tia voiced her assent and waited. A quick vote followed.

Not surprisingly, the second suggestion got the most votes, although two of her classmates lobbied hard for the public burning of his property.

Take away what he wants most.

Tia frowned when the message popped into the mailbox three more times in quick succession. Who are you? she typed. Identify yourself.

When the author of the messages stayed silent, Debbie posted the official total, and the tattooing won. Relieved, Tia sat back and waited. Somebody would have to plan how they'd trick Gary so that he'd be at their mercy enough for them to accomplish their goal.

All the women in the class chatted back and forth, suggestions flying.

Tia scanned them, then leaned forward when she saw her name mentioned. **Tia, your job will be to distract Byron.**

Apparently, he'd made it a point to contact each of the women and let them know that the police were there for them—and their spouses—if the need arose.

Byron had made it clear that the department wouldn't tolerate any acts of revenge. Several of the women chimed in that they supported Ginger and would do whatever was necessary, short of getting arrested.

When? Tia typed.

Starting today.

Tia ran her fingers through her hair, then held her stomach, feeling a sudden case of nerves. It wasn't as if she hadn't been alone with Byron, she just hadn't *had* to be alone with him.

Besides, he'd been right. They had decided to go after Ginger's husband. But they'd been talking silly stuff until tonight. Max out his credit cards and send out company e-mails about his nonsexual abilities, nothing like the ominous-sounding e-mails that had come through earlier. She was glad that nobody had wanted to act on those suggestions.

Closing her eyes, Tia inhaled deeply and reflected on her life with her ex. She stopped a minute. That was a first. She hadn't ever categorized Dante that way before. It felt good. Tia knew she'd moved another step away from their past and let her thoughts flow.

They'd been happy for a time, but unhappy for far longer. He was gone now. She didn't know where and didn't care.

Dante had wanted a certain lifestyle, and now neither of them had it. What a mess they'd made.

Yet the end was near. Now that she'd stopped wanting to hurt him, she'd slept comfortably last night. Better, in fact, than she had in a while. And her stomach didn't have its customary burn.

The thought consoled her. One day soon she'd be sitting at home, in front of her fireplace, and she would look back on these days and be thankful they hadn't lasted forever.

Work had been agonizingly slow this week, with no storms brewing over the Pacific or the Atlantic. The wildfires in Oklahoma had been doused, and it had stopped snowing in California.

Even the volcanoes were sleeping, yet the hair on the back of her neck stood up. She turned around and met Chance's smoldering glare.

"Surfing the net on company time?"

"Yes, I am."

"Another violation," Chance purred, change tinkling in her hand. "Make it easy on yourself and resign."

"Why should I? I do my work, I come in on time, and I give more than a hundred percent to this company. I'm not quitting, Chance, although I know that would be easier for you since you already promised my job to someone's niece."

"You sneaky little witch. Lurking in bathrooms now? That's a new low, even for you."

"I was using the facilities. Perhaps you should think about that before you start a personal conversation in a public latrine."

"I-I," Chance said, stumbling over her words.

"I'm heading to the Hilton, you care to join me?"

"I don't fraternize, Tia. I keep business and my personal life separate."

"I understand. I was there a couple weeks ago and saw a woman get the piss slapped out of her. Made me wonder how a businesswoman could get caught up in being a victim. I thought I'd mention it in case we were looking for an expose-type story. The women behind domestic abuse."

Chance's milky white face was splotchy and red. "I don't know anything about that. And thank you very much, but we have real reporters and producers who can come up with stories without your help. Just quit, dammit!"

Tia clicked the mouse three times in succession, then squeezed past Chance. "No can do."

Tia grabbed the papers from the printer outside her cube and handed them to her boss. "This is a satellite view of Earth and its alignment to the moon. A tsunami might result. You never know. This is a satellite photo from a week ago, monitoring the gasses that surpassed the Earth's atmosphere from the fires out West. And this is the forecast for the next five days. I'm not sure, but I think I'm doing my job. Probable cause for firing me? I don't think so, but we might want to run it by the station's attorneys."

"This isn't a right to work state, Tia. I can fire you for any reason I please."

Tia glared at the pale-faced woman, tired of her,

tired of the threats, and tired of being tired. She needed her job, but she didn't need the harassment.

"What's stopping you? You seem to enjoy coming around, holding this job over me. I overheard you on the phone basically giving my job away. If it's like that, then why am I still here?"

To her credit, Chance's face became mottled. "My parents seem to think you're worth saving."

"That can't be it. You relish your authority but don't seem to quite have all your fingers on the big girl switch that will seal my fate."

"Chance, why don't you tell Tia the real reason you can't just up and terminate her?" Ronnie/Rhonda said, coming from the side cube, making both women jump.

Dressed in a hot pink shirt and slimming black pants, he looked like he was ready to be lord of the dance or something. Despite his unannounced arrival, Tia was grateful for his presence. She needed a friend. Lately, all hers seemed to need a lot of counseling.

Rhonda/Ronnie's question lingered.

"What are you still doing here? All the gay bars in Atlanta closed?" Chance insulted her brother in a mildly irritated voice, her straight black brows crinkled at the very ends. How did she do that?

Rhonda/Ronnie growled at his sister, yet his expression was gentle. "My date's picking me up in a bit, darling. Then we're going to paint this town fuchsia." He laughed at her wince. "Now that I've answered your question, you answer mine. Why don't you tell Tia why haven't you fired her?"

"That's none of her business."

Tia didn't agree. "You harass me all day. You

sneak around, stand over my shoulder, go through my desk, and try to intimidate me. I do my job. I'm about finished with the class. I don't know what more you want."

"The desk is company property," Chance shot back.

"You're avoiding again," Ronnie/Rhonda chimed in. "Tia, Chance can't fire you because she has to have a two-thirds vote from the owners—meaning three of the four of us must agree before she can terminate an employee. Right now, she doesn't have that."

"Ultimately, I have the final decision," Chance said. "If you don't perform to standard, you will be terminated, and these"—she held up the papers Tia'd given her moments ago—"aren't going to cut it."

"What are those?" Ronnie/Rhonda asked casually.

Chance glanced at the papers. "Aerial photos of the earth. Elementary stuff."

"But part of the duties you assigned to her. I'd have to testify to the fact that she gave you what you asked for. Good night, sis. Sleep well."

Chance stomped off, and Tia gave Ronnie/Rhonda a big hug.

"I didn't get fired and not realize it, did I?" Tia asked.

"No, cream puff," he said, with a sad smile and serious eyes. "You were saved by the big, gay wolf."

This time his growl made her laugh. "That gay wolf is my hero. I just hope I'm not creating a rift in your family."

Ronnie/Rhonda laughed fully. He grabbed her sweater and doused the light on her desk. "Honey, you couldn't touch our troubles if you crocheted together all the Neide Ambrosio belts in the world. Do your job, and you'll come out on top."

They rode the elevator down in companionable silence, Ronnie/Rhonda swinging her hand.

"How is Officer Abs, Ass, and Pecs?" he asked.

Tia giggled, some of the tension leaving her. All day her whole body had been tight with tension, but now that she was off duty, she felt as if she were emerging from an iceberg. "He's fine. We're not a couple, you know. He's just my—"

"Bodyguard?" Ronnie/Rhonda filled in. "Like Kevin Costner to Whitney Houston? Like Taye Diggs to Angela Bassett? Like Larenz Tate to Nia Long? Like—"

"No," Tia interrupted. "You know your movies, don't you?"

Ronnie/Rhonda checked his manicured fingernails. "It's chapter six in the being bi man's handbook."

"You're so silly." They walked outside as Tia shouldered on her jacket, loving the slow slide from winter to spring. The sun had already set in the west, but a few fingers of orange and blue streaked the sky in the distance. She wanted to head in that direction and chase the tail end of the day, but reconsidered when her stomach growled for food.

Ronnie/Rhonda stood next to her in his sleek outfit, looking like he should be on somebody's drill team. She wasn't sure, however, what college would have pink as its school color. "Who is this mystery man, and is he on the way?"

Checking a beautiful Movado watch, Ronnie/ Rhonda nodded. "He's Damien St. Jacques. Sounds like a porn star, but he's not. He's with an accounting firm, and yes, he'll be here in about five minutes. Would you like to join us for dinner?"

Tia blushed. Ronnie/Rhonda really was her friend. "You don't need a chaperone. Have a good time, and I don't want to hear a single detail tomorrow. You know, I'm still in relationship recovery."

He grinned big. "Please, cream puff, you're over Mr. Stupid. I'm tellin' you every last lip-smackin', booty-rubbin', chest-touchin'—"

Tia cried out, laughing as Ronnie/Rhonda pretended to molest her on the street. The sidewalk cleared around them as smiling people gave them room to play.

"Behave," she told him as the wind blew her hair into her face. She wiped the curls away. "You're never going to get a second date if he sees you feeling me up."

"Oh, damn. I didn't think of that. She's a lesbian!" Ronnie/Rhonda announced to passersby. "She's trying to turn me," he said to two obviously gay men.

"Into what, baby? A boy?" the tall thin man said.

Tia and Ronnie/Rhonda joined the men in uninhibited laughter. The men winked and walked on down the street.

When she could control herself, Tia patted Ronnie/Rhonda's arm. "I've got to go now. My bus will be coming soon."

"Where's your car?"

"Parked until I can afford to drive it."

She saw the look on his face and rubbed his arm. He was feeling sorry for her, and she wasn't going to have it.

"Hey, I'm fine. Man, I can stand to lose a few

pounds," she said. "Walking to and from the bus stop isn't going to hurt me."

"Tia, it's dinner, and it's not an imposition. I don't want you trolling happy hours for free food anymore."

"I don't do that." Tia turned her embarrassed face in the opposite direction of Ronnie/Rhonda's. How did he know? She'd been so discreet. Perhaps he'd seen her. Or it could be that every doggie bag in the break-room refrigerator had her name on it. "I'm going to have spaghetti—" she lied.

"Tia, is that you? Remember me? It's Kirk."

Distant reminders tickled her memory. Tia looked up into the handsome face of Kirk Giles.

"Right," she said, extending her hand. "This is my friend Rhonda/Ronnie!" The men shook, and to Tia's relief, Kirk didn't seem at all homophobic.

They'd met at happy hour a while back, and Tia was supposed to have called him. Somehow she hadn't gotten around to it. Her life sucked, and she hadn't wanted to share that bad news.

"What are you doing over here?" she asked.

He grinned, showing a perfect Crest white smile. "I ran into your friend Megan, and she said you were waiting for her to pick you up. So I offered, hoping we could grab a bite to eat and talk."

Alarms went off in Tia's head. She wasn't waiting for Megan. "Where'd you see my friend?"

"At Art & More on Ponce this afternoon."

One of Ronnie/Rhonda's eyebrows shot up like Chance's, and Tia caught his drift. What successful, gainfully employed brotha went to an art store in the middle of the day? One who'd just lost a job or was *about* to lose one.

Kirk gave them a knowing smile. "I'm in radio. They're running a promo ad, and while we're still a small start-up, I wanted to press the flesh and get to know the area at the same time. I assure you both, I have a *real* nine-to-five job."

All three laughed. Atlanta was full of fakers.

"We believe you," Ronnie/Rhonda said to Kirk. "Press the flesh," he sighed to Tia. "Yum."

Tia elbowed Ronnie/Rhonda. "That sounds great," she said to Kirk. "I wonder what Megan was doing there."

"She said something about finishing a mural."

Tia rolled her eyes but couldn't comment further. The girl was definitely certifiable.

Just then a sleek, smoke grey Lexus convertible pulled to the curb, and a pretty blond man stretched out of the vehicle, leaning on the door and the roof. "You ready?"

"Double yum. Good night, girls and boys." Rhonda/Ronnie kissed Tia's temple and looked directly at Kirk. "Tia's the absolute best meteorologist in the state. Don't try to steal her away from us. And don't break her heart."

The men shook hands firmly. "I'll take good care of her," said Kirk.

Ronnie/Rhonda leaned over Tia, fixing her already straightened collar, and said, "Don't look now, but Officer Wonderful is fuming over your left shoulder."

He started humming Nelly's "Hot in Herre" before climbing into the Lexus. The men drove away, leaving Tia and Kirk in the middle of the block.

"Want to grab a bite to eat?" Kirk asked.

So Byron was spying?

She might as well give him something to look at. "Best offer I've had all day."

Although Tia wanted to look over her shoulder, she couldn't bring herself. Lately, she'd been having more than just feelings for the attentive cop. She'd been dreaming about him.

Wanting to hear his voice. Imagining them together. And she wasn't happy about it.

He'd arrested her. Carried her out of jail over his shoulder. Shoved her into his police cruiser, and in general, had been arrogant and bossy.

She wondered if she suffered from some type of bizarre attachment disorder. Like Stockholm syndrome.

Some people fell in love with their therapists. Others with their doctor.

Maybe she was infatuated with Byron because he was the only man who'd paid her any attention lately. Byron was her protector. There was comfort in knowing he was just over her shoulder, watchin' her ass.

Tia didn't look back as she added a little more sway to her step.

She took Kirk's extended arm. "I'm incredibly hungry. What did you have in mind?"

"I'd love some soul food. Know of a good place around here?"

"Gladys Knight's restaurant. It's called Chicken and Waffles. They have a full menu. Want to give it a try?"

"Lead the way." Kirk gave her an admiring glance that said he would let her lead, for now.

She got into his Infiniti and belted in. Looking at his navigational system, she plugged in the street name and address, and they both looked right before he eased into traffic. Then Tia drew back.

A squad car had pulled door to door with their vehicle, and a scowling black man was staring at her.

"What's he doing?" Kirk asked.

Tia met Byron's stare evenly.

What was he doing? Was he jealous that she was with another man?

There was no class tonight. So he couldn't say she'd be late or that he was there to offer her a ride. Maybe he thought Kirk was involved in her plot to retaliate against Ginger's husband.

Kirk put the car in park. "Maybe he thinks I pulled into traffic illegally. I hate cops who take their jobs too seriously. Maybe if you smile at him, he'll be nice."

"It'll take more than that. Believe me."

Byron turned away and started moving his mouth. As he talked, she admired the shift of his jaw, the way it clenched and relaxed as he spoke. She studied it now as she had a hundred times before.

He looked at her suddenly, gave her a two-fingered salute that looked more like a warning, then pulled off, taking the corner ahead in a hurry.

What had taken him away so quickly? Tia didn't want to acknowledge the feeling of disappointment in her stomach. Although she hadn't been expecting Byron, it was nice knowing he'd been there.

"He's gone," she said.

"Don't sound so disappointed. That smile worked like magic."

"Okay, we need to have an understanding. I'm in relationship recovery. So if your intentions are anything more than friendship, you should probably take me to the bus stop—after we stop at Chicken and Waffles and get me something to eat."

Kirk gave her a long look before they both burst out laughing.

"Yeah?" he asked, following the directions of the automated voice.

"Yeah," Tia confirmed.

"Then let's get you some food, enjoy some friendly conversation and nothing more. Sound good to you?"

"Perfect."

Tia swallowed the last of her food and laughed when Kirk eyed her plate.

"You want something else?" he asked.

"Don't ask. You might have to get a job washing dishes. I might eat a hole in your wallet."

He pretended to wince and smiled. He would be perfect for Megan if she wasn't so strange right now. "My wallet can handle it. After all you've told me about your job, why don't you just quit? You can get something else. You're certainly marketable."

"You heard Rhonda/Ronnie. I'm supposedly the best." Tia didn't really believe all his hype, but a part of her wanted to. "I've never walked away from anything. I can't now."

"Tia, there's no shame in leaving a job that's no longer working for you. That's the thing about options. I think of them as coins." He pulled a handful from his pocket and showed them to her. "See these? All different sizes and colors. When you need them, you pick what's best, what's right for that time."

She smiled. "Good analogy. I guess I'm just not there yet."

"Then you should fulfill your destiny. I'm proud of you for not bailing out. If you ever change your mind, consider radio. We could use a good weather, traffic, full-time whatever we need you to be person."

Tia smiled at the vague but all-inclusive job description. Lately, her job had turned into a girl Friday–type thing, and although not what she wanted, it was far more interesting than just editing weather copy for Ben.

"Thanks, Kirk. I'll keep an open mind." Her cell phone interrupted the life lesson, and Tia picked up. "Hello?"

"It's Sonny."

"Oh. Hey. What are you doing calling me?" Tia sat up straight, the shine rubbing off an otherwise enjoyable evening.

"Megan's here again. At my house."

Tia wondered why she should give a rip but was reminded of the last picture Megan had painted of Sonny's severed penis. "What's she doing?"

"Sitting on the porch."

"Why? I mean, has she said anything?"

"Only that she wants to talk to me."

"Have you talked to her?"

"Do you know what she looks like? Like she came straight out of living in Grant Park. She's covered in paint. And she smells."

"Damn, Sonny. Four weeks ago you were engaged to the girl, and now you're married to someone else. Excuse Megan for not being able to make the transition as quickly as you."

Kirk paid their check and picked up Tia's jacket.

She edged out of her seat. "What are you doing?" she asked as he ushered her from the restaurant.

"We're going to get your friend."

Tia hesitated, then nodded. "Okay."

"Tia," Sonny said in her ear, "you're her girl, and maybe you can talk some sense into her. Come get her. This is the last time. If it happens again, I'm calling the cops." Sonny hung up.

"What a jerk," Kirk said. Tia hurried alongside him as they half jogged through the parking lot to the car. "I take it that was her ex."

"Yeah, a real winner. He broke up with her, married another woman the next day, and Megan hasn't taken it too well."

"She didn't look like herself earlier, but I figured she was an artist. They can look rather strange. I still thought she was cute."

She gave him an odd look. "Yeah, well, she isn't an artist but should be, and this is strange for her. She's been working as a corrections officer for the past four years, until she got put on leave three weeks ago." Tia fell silent.

"And?" he asked.

"I shouldn't be telling you this. Megan's my girl. I feel like I'm being disloyal." She gave him directions, but otherwise, they stayed quiet for a while.

"How about this?" he finally said. "I've suffered from bipolar disorder for five years now. It's rare, but I have my bad times, too. You're a good friend, Tia. When I met you I got that feeling."

They pulled onto Sonny's street and up to the house.

Megan was sitting on the porch, her head resting

on her knees. A woman sat beside her, patting her back. Sonny was nowhere to be found.

Tia approached slowly, looking between the pair. "Hey, Meg. How are you, sweetie?"

"Fine. I came by to return something."

Tia looked around and didn't see a bag of any kind. Megan had probably had a water/paint moment. "Did you give it to . . ." Tia looked at the woman next to her friend.

"I'm Vivian. Sonny's wife," said the woman, mouthing the last two words.

Tia gave her the once-over. She was all right. Not as cute as her friend, but with a quiet confidence and calm air about her, which warred with the situation. "Did you give your package to Vivian?" Tia asked.

Megan rubbed her eyes. "I forgot it. Tia, I did a stupid thing coming over here."

Tia didn't say anything but extended her hand to her friend. Rain splattered her hand and wrist. "You ready to go home?"

Megan looked at Vivian. "She mentioned a place I might go for a little time off. There's people I can talk to. Maybe help me move on."

Vivian handed Tia a card, and Tia and Kirk helped Megan up. They walked slowly to his car, and Vivian hugged Megan, who couldn't stop crying. "You're going to be fine. When you're well, we'll talk," whispered Vivian.

With Megan and Kirk in the backseat of the car, Tia turned to Sonny's wife. "You're so nice to her. Why?"

"She needed compassion. I don't blame her. Please make sure she gets help. I made a call to the Atlanta Psychiatric Center. They're expecting her."

"How convenient."

"It's her choice, Tia. I understand your concern, and I know how this looks."

"You do?"

"Yes," Vivian said, nodding. "I do."

All the fight in Tia flew away, and her stomach settled a bit. She stood there a moment, so many questions running through her head, she had to ask at least one. "How long have you known Sonny?"

"All my life. We grew up across the street from one another. It was love from knee-high. Relationships came and went, and I'm just sorry she got caught in the crosshairs of our love drama. Neither Sonny nor I handled this well. Seeing her like this proves we could have done things a lot differently. I'm here if you need me."

"Thank you, Dr. Ellis."

She smiled gently. "Just Vivian."

After Tia was in bed at Megan's that night, the events of the day wouldn't stop running through her head. She'd started in one way and ended in another.

The whole thing was just—she searched for the appropriate word—bizarre. Bizarre was the only one that would fit.

First, Megan had painted the walls, then Tia'd sold two purses, received unexpected support from Rhonda/Ronnie, had dinner with Kirk, rescued Megan, and then had a frank conversation with Vivian.

Tia never, ever, thought she and "the other woman" would share a moment of camaraderie, let alone a common goal of Megan's better health, and now as she lay alone in bed, unable to sleep, all she could think about was sharing the events of her day with Byron.

Tia wasn't sure what to think.

She glanced at her cell phone and noted the time. Byron worked until seven in the morning. He was up now, and so was she. Unable to resist, she dialed and couldn't help the sting of disappointment at getting his voice mail.

"I saw you today," she said, and cringed. That wasn't what she'd wanted to say. She didn't want to sound accusatory. Actually, she was flattered that she'd invited him to watch her ass, and he did. It was ego boosting at a time when her ego had more holes than a political alibi.

A growing part of her wanted to pursue the lustful looks he often tried to conceal.

"Today was strange," she continued. "I just thought I'd share that with you. Okay. I sold two purses. You don't care about that. Okay. Bye. Don't call me back." She blinked at the ridiculous statement. "I hope I already said good-bye."

Tia turned over and hollered into her pillow. "Damn, damn, damn. That was the dumbest phone call ever. He's going to think you're crazy."

The phone beeped twice.

Tia looked at the receiver in her hand. In her tiny tantrum, she'd just hung up. Crap. He'd heard everything.

She dropped the phone and closed her eyes. If she fell asleep, in her dreams she'd probably get eaten by a dinosaur. Somehow that seemed better than facing Byron tomorrow.

Chapter Nineteen

Byron changed the battery in his cell phone and swore under his breath. The damned thing wasn't working again. Yesterday he'd gotten messages from three days ago and none today. He sat in his squad car, trying to get the back off the cell phone, when his radio beeped.

"Officer Rivers responding, over."

"A message from your sister. Your cell phone isn't working. Are you okay?"

Byron stared out into the dark night and shook his head in disbelief. "Tell Camilla *again* that she can't use the police department dispatcher to let me know my cell phone isn't working, which I already know. I don't care if she is married to my former chief's son. I'll call her when I get home in the morning."

The dispatcher laughed. "Copy that. She said thanks for the late Christmas present. Something about the bag being perfect. Major Snell out."

Byron disconnected the call and put his car in gear. He'd heard the guys in the back laughing, but he didn't care. His baby sister was a princess who'd never struggled a day in her life. She'd met and married the chief's son ten years ago, and they were as happy today as they'd been the day they'd met. And although she was married, Byron had never gotten over spoiling her. Perhaps if he had a woman of his own, he'd be different.

He stopped at the all-night gas station on Fourteenth and went inside.

"Hey, Prakash. Good night tonight?"

"Very well, Atlanta's finest."

"I need to use your phone please."

"Sure, Byron. But only if you stop the rain," the clerk joked, a happy smile splitting his face. The older man had been in Atlanta twenty years but hadn't lost his heavy Indian accent.

"I'll make a call." Byron winked and folded his hands as if to pray.

Prakash was definitely a praying man. He grinned bigger. "Then I'll buzz you in. Your cell phone not working again?"

Byron groaned. "No and no. I'm not buying one of those rip-off joints you sell. I'll go to the cellular store tomorrow and get a replacement."

Prakash giggled. "You insult me *and* want to use my phone. I think that will cost extra."

Byron smiled back at the man as he dialed his cell number and listened to his messages. Tia's message sounded discombobulated, but it was good to hear her wanting to share with him rather than keep secrets. He noted the time and saw that only thirty minutes had passed.

It must have been a long day if she was still awake at this odd hour.

Seeing her earlier with another man had stoked jealous embers he'd thought long gone, but obviously there were not. The jealous feelings had reminded him that he was still a healthy man with unfulfilled needs.

Although Tia sounded tired, she was probably still awake.

He dialed her number, and she answered on the first ring.

"Tia Amberson."

"Byron. How bad was your day?"

The question sounded intimate, as if they'd been sharing these intimate details for years. He and Tia fought but, in some ways, knew more about each other than most couples.

Ever since she'd invited him to watch her, he'd become a student of her life. He knew how she took her burgers and that she liked to window-shop the day before payday. She loved Victoria's Secret panties and expensive shoes. She would close her eyes and throw back her head at the taste of rich dark chocolate, which she sampled only when it was offered by the Godiva lady in the mall, and he now knew why she waited to catch the 7:15 bus and got off on Courtland on Wednesdays.

The Sheraton had a happy hour that ended at eight, and she'd befriended the chef, who always had a plate ready for her if she did one thing. She had to kiss the old man on the cheek.

Tia would take the plate, give him a kiss, and catch the 8:10 bus home. The driver would accept her transfer, if she sat in the front seat and showed him a little leg.

She was sexy, humorous, curious, and fearless.

And she'd called to share that with him. He felt himself getting hard just thinking about her.

"How bad was your day?" he repeated.

"I thought you were somebody from work," she said, letting her voice relax.

"I can hang up if you're resting."

"No, my day was so bad that I can't sleep, so I got up, and I'm having a glass of wine. I take it you got my message."

"Yes. I won't hold that message against you."

She chuckled. "Thank goodness."

"Nothing wrong with the house, I hope?"

"No. No new break-ins to report, Officer."

"I'm relieved," he said and chuckled. Her silence troubled him. Usually, she'd have something smart to say. "New trouble with Manuel?"

"No."

"Your roommate?"

"Ding, ding. You hit the jackpot."

He could hear her sipping her wine in the silence. "Sounds rough," he added.

"Ended not so great, but it wasn't that awful." Her voice said otherwise, but he didn't push. "What number is this?" she asked.

"I'm at a store."

"The grocery store?"

"No. Well, they have groceries. It's a convenience store."

"Leave it to you to be specific," she said, with a chuckle. "I would kill for some cheese Pringles."

"I have lunch coming up in about ten minutes. Care to join me?"

"It's three forty-five in the morning," she said, sounding just shy of incredulous. "Aren't you on duty?"

"I am, but I have food. I can stop by, unless you've got a better offer or company."

He was digging, he knew. But he had to know. Had to hear in her voice if the man he'd seen her with earlier was her new man.

The sound of pattering rain filled the short silence. "I'm alone." Her voice dropped an octave, to a sexy depth of truth and promise.

"Cheese?" he asked, his heart racing.

"That's right."

"See you in ten minutes."

"Ten, it is," she said and hung up.

Byron paid for his selections and was on his way in two minutes. Outside her place by 3:58 a.m., he knocked, his shoulders hunched to keep the rain from running down his neck. When Tia opened the door, he got a good glimpse of her. Long Tweety Bird pajama bottoms and a spaghetti-strap top hardly covered her womanly shape.

"Hey," he said, soaking in the sight of her, with her hair down and her body relaxed.

"How long do you have for lunch?" she asked.

"Forty-five minutes."

"Okay," she said, barely meeting his gaze. "Come in."

Byron couldn't help but watch the sway of her hips as she walked into the living room. The paintings that had dominated the walls were now gone. No more hatchet in the private area. No more emasculated men. "Hey." He turned, noting the difference. "The walls—"

"They knocked down the center wall to make this into one big room. Megan wanted more of a studio feel."

"So where is Megan?"

"Atlanta Psychiatric Center."

"Wow." Byron gazed at her. "You can't just say that and leave me hanging. What happened?"

"She went over to Sonny's house."

"Her ex?"

"Right."

"Oh. Okay. Well, did everything end okay?"

Byron opened his bag lunch on the kitchen counter, on a paper towel Tia handed him. A film of dust covered the surfaces, except where she'd shown him to unpack his lunch. In the few minutes she'd had before his arrival, she'd tried to tidy up a bit.

Her hair was still sleep tossed, but she'd cleaned off the counter and uncovered a chair for him. The rest were stacked in the corner, draped with heavy clear plastic.

Tia leaned back against the sink and put her arm under her breasts and her wineglass to her lips.

"Why do you think things didn't end well?" she asked. "Everybody isn't trying to commit a crime, you know. You are not the only law-abiding citizen of this world."

"I never said that." Byron offered her half his sandwich.

She refused. "I know—"

He sat down on the chair, bit, chewed, and swallowed. "I see the worst of people, Tia. It's natural for me to think that something might have happened. So straighten me out. Isn't that what you want to do? Tell me something good came from your best friend being locked up in the Atlanta Psychiatric Center."

She sipped her wine. "She went over to Sonny's house to give him something. I have no idea what, but we both know she was a bit off yesterday.

Anyway, I was having dinner with a friend, and I got a call from Sonny that Megan was at his house and to come get her."

Tia grew quiet, and Byron kept his emotions to himself.

Jealousy tightened his jaw even as he ate his food, but he found solace in the fact that at this hour of the morning, she was sharing a meal with him.

He took another bite of his meat loaf sandwich and chewed.

She poured him a glass of water from the refrigerator, and he drank. Their fingers touched, and he promised himself that if he touched her again, tonight wouldn't end in a platonic manner. "How did she end up at the APC?"

"It turns out Sonny's wife, Vivian, is a psychiatrist. She spent time with Megan, and by the time I got there, she was sitting on the porch, comforting Megan. Vivian suggested Megan go to APC and talk to someone." Tia shrugged. "Megan agreed."

"You were okay with that?"

"Yeah." She said the word as if it were a question, then began to look worried. "That was the right thing to do, right? Megan's going to be fine. I didn't let her sign herself in for life, did I? I shouldn't have trusted Vivian, should I have? She's the other woman. Oh, my goodness! I'm supposed to be looking out for Megan's best interests, and I'm listening the woman who stole her man. Crap!"

"Tia, don't do this."

Tia dropped her wineglass into the sink and was almost at the front door when Byron snagged her wrist. "Tia, Megan is where she needs to be."

"What if she changed her mind? What if she

thinks I put her there? She's going to be mad as hell. I have to go get her. I don't have many friends." Her voice broke. "I mean I need her—"

Byron pulled Tia close, her back against the wall, and closed his mouth over hers. She struggled for a second; then her upper body pressed into his bulletproof vest.

As much as the vest was supposed to protect, it was powerless against the effect of Tia's passion. He felt her heat, desire, and wanting. It seeped in between his second and third rib and spread like a virus until his whole body was bent into her like a sunflower to the sun.

His mouth scoured hers, their tongues tangling in the first steps of mating. "She'll be fine," he kept hearing himself say, until Tia kissed him into urgent, passionate silence.

Lightning and thunder shook the town house, and Byron took that to mean no matter how much he wanted Tia, he had to let her go.

Tia was as tumultuous and bold as thunder, as unpredictable as lightning. She was not a woman he needed to handle on a daily basis. Making love to her now would lead them further down a road that ultimately was a dead end. But it didn't have to be a dead end, his subconscious told him.

Byron leaned his forehead against hers, their breath moving between them.

Don't look at me, he silently pleaded.

Her eyes could force him to his knees.

She tipped her head sideways, looked up, and licked his lips. Then she bit him.

Byron nearly lost it.

He took her hips in his hands. Damn, he did enjoy the contents of her Tweety Bird pajamas.

His lips trailed down her neck, and she leaned to the side, giving him better access.

He was strong, he told himself. He could leave her alone.

Summoning all his willpower, Byron gave her bottom one final, extended caress. "I'd better get going."

Tia's fingers began a tuneless song on his neck. She acted as if she didn't hear him. "You just got here. You've got at least thirty-five minutes. Stay at least another fifteen."

He hardened. "Tia, nothing with me is fifteen minutes short."

"I'll remember that," she said honestly, her hands trying futilely to find an entrance point to his skin. When she couldn't get to him, she used another tactic.

Her left leg played tricks with the back of his legs while she moved his right hand to the heart-shaped curve of her bottom.

His hand naturally contracted in place. "That's a little better," she murmured. "How about this?"

She placed his other hand at her waist, eased up the bottom of her pajama top, and exposed the cranberry center of her nipple. Then she gave him a come hither smile.

His mouth watered.

Perching on her toes, Tia wound her arms around his neck. Her tongue darted out and laved his lips in one slow, convincing lick.

Byron slid both hands inside her pajama pants,

cupped her bottom, and raised her higher. Nothing in the world felt better than this.

"Strip," she told him.

There were rules regarding how one's lunch hour was supposed to be used. Byron was aware of every one of them. But he'd been following rules all his life, and they'd gotten him exactly where he was right now: at the crossroads between right and wrong.

Tia kissed him until his thoughts were as scrambled as the letters on the Soul Train letter board.

"I should go," he said.

"You're on your lunch break."

"I'm not eating, Tia," he reminded her.

"You could be," Tia informed him innocently. "I'm quite delicious. I taste like desire and satisfaction."

Another level of control snapped. Byron tried to raise another weak objection when Tia licked his lips again. He tried again, and she licked him again.

He forgot why he was trying to leave and what he was trying to say. All he could think about was the woman in his arms, and how this next step felt almost natural.

"Are you hungry, Officer Rivers?"

Byron felt himself melting, like brown sugar under a steady stream of warm water. "Extremely."

"Then you'll stay with me," she said softly, as if the decision were up to her alone. She encouraged his fingers to caress her breast.

Byron guided her closer. "We don't have much time. I have to leave soon. That wouldn't be fair."

Tia licked him again, and this time, her tongue made sensual love to his until he was not only befuddled, but breathless. Her mouth trailed down his jaw to his neck, where she stopped at his Adam's apple. His head fell against hers, and she kept up her sensual assault, leaving tiny, wet kisses under his chin, then going back to his mouth.

Byron throbbed against her, and he realized he held her so tightly against him, it was a wonder that she could breathe, let alone seduce him.

"Don't worry about being fair to me," she finally whispered.

"Why?" he asked.

"I'm getting mine right now. Leaving," she said sassily, "won't be fair to you."

Byron didn't think it was possible to get any harder than he was, but he felt as if all the blood in his body were centered between his legs.

"My room is the last door on the left."

Byron carried Tia down the hall and laid her gently on the bed. It took him just a couple of minutes to unbuckle and undress.

He turned and stopped.

Tia was still clad in her Tweety bird pajamas. "They're nice," he said, "but not how I imagined us at this point." He kneeled on the bed beside her.

"I thought you'd like to unwrap your special gift."

Byron pulled Tia by her foot and stripped her naked.

"I always enjoy the wrapping," he explained, as he explored her body with his tongue, making her shake with uncontrollable pleasure. "But I always enjoy what's inside more."

Splaying her on the bed, Byron found he loved the delicious contours of the body he'd dreamed about countless nights. Tia's body was shapely, her skin so soft he would have been content to taste her until the early morning light.

He kissed her stomach, the inside of her thighs, the soles of her feet, her mouth. Every bit of her intrigued him, and Byron wanted to make love to Tia in such a way that her mind and body remembered him forever.

Leaning up, he caressed her until his name came from her mouth in breathless pants. He lavished kisses on her breasts and neck, giving her pleasure. Then his mouth touched the center of her body. Her legs moved restlessly.

Tia was his. "Turn over," he told her.

She rolled onto her stomach, trusting him, spreading her legs. Tia whimpered as he reached beneath her, caressing her G-spot.

He loved the sounds she made, the tiny sighs, the moans and groans of pleasure, the way she whispered his name, and the way she cried "Yeeeeesss" when she came. Even her purr of satisfaction after her orgasm made his heart go flip-flop.

"Condom?" Byron asked.

Tia slid on her belly to the edge of the bed and pulled a packet of five from the drawer.

"That's ambitious," he told her, with a smile, as he rolled one on.

"Then we'd better get back to it."

Tia climbed into his lap, and as their bodies joined, their gazes met and held. For every second that he looked into her eyes, his heart equated that to ten years that he would love her.

Byron trusted that emotion and lost all concept of time, wanting to stay with her forever.

Looking down at their union, he saw that she was indeed shaved clean, and inexplicably, he grew harder.

A guttural laugh came from her throat. "You're going to split me in two."

"We can stop," he said, her nipples grazing his lips.

"Not on your life."

"Good," he breathed into her mouth. "That's good."

He lowered his hand and began to stroke her. Tia started to climax, one wave after another. She cried out, her mouth devouring his, her nails raking his body, until he felt himself climbing the mountain to bliss.

"Harder," she cried.

Byron moved faster, deeper; then Tia surprised him and clamped his sex with hers.

Reason failed him, and his plan for taking her *there* one more time blew away as a magnificent orgasm thrust him over the edge.

Chapter Twenty

Tia spun her chair around at work, a smile pulling at the corners of her mouth. Life was good. Even through the hardship and all she'd been through, life was finally getting better.

Her cell phone beeped, and she grabbed it. "Tia Amberson."

"Hey, it's me."

"Megan? How are you, Sweetie?"

"Fine. Getting better. You?'"

"Good. Really good."

"Since you have my house to yourself, right?"

Tia smiled. "I'd rather you be there, too. How are you?"

"Good. I think I'm going to come home in the next day or two."

"That's great news. I'll pick you up. What time?"

"Well, actually, I have a ride."

"Oh," Tia said, crestfallen. Maybe Megan was upset about Tia not breaking her out of the APC. "So Rachel is going to bring you home. I'll grab some Chinese food."

"I haven't heard from Rachel, but, well, it's Kirk."

"Kirk?" Tia sat up straight, and a gentle smile softened her voice. "You go crazy and get a hunk. Dang, girl. You got skills."

Megan laughed, sounding like her old self. "I haven't talked to him. We're not really allowed contact from the outside. I got all your messages, though. I really appreciate you taking care of me the way you did."

"Meg, you're my girl. If you're having a bad day, I am, too. I'm there for you. So, what's the deal with Kirk?"

"I haven't seen him since I got here, but every day he brings flowers and leaves me a note. Nothing serious. Just that he'd like to be my friend. Yesterday he said he got a ticket for almost causing a traffic accident. He let a squirrel cross the road."

Tia and Megan burst out laughing.

"Aw. He's got a good heart," said Tia.

"He's so not from Georgia," Megan replied, sounding just like her old self. "Now you know, if I'd said that to Rachel, she'd be quoting some statistics about how squirrels cause accidents and kill people."

Tia chuckled. Rachel always had been full of shit.

"You talked to her?" Megan asked.

"No," Tia replied, "and I don't want to talk about her now. Hey, Meg, I need to ask you something. Seriously."

"Shoot. Then I have to go. I have group therapy in ten minutes, and I need to go wash my face. What's up?"

"Did you go to my old place and get my other purses?"

"First, it's not your old place. It's *your* place, period. Second, yes, I did."

Tia closed her eyes. On the one hand, she was grateful to her friend, but Megan could have gotten her in a lot of trouble.

"I know it was wrong, and you don't have to worry about me getting into your business again," said Megan. "I've learned I need to read all the signs that are happening in my life and stay focused on me. Did you want to say something, Tia?"

Tia exhaled as she looked at her computer screen. She had mail from her anger management friends.

"Enough has been said, friend. So you think tomorrow is the big day for you to come home?"

"Yes. The food here is lousy. Don't forget about the Chinese. No MSG. It could interact with these new meds I've been put on."

For someone who'd never had a sick day from work, Megan sure was handling her mental situation with maturity and class.

In a way, Tia felt shame at her reaction to her breakup with Dante. Then she remembered all that had happened to get Megan to this point.

She realized they'd traveled different roads but were where they were supposed to be.

"I'll see you tomorrow, Megan. Take care of yourself."

"Thanks, Tia. Hey!"

"What is it, Sweetie?"

"I love you. I never say that, and I should."

Tia's eyes teared. "Me, too. Bye," she whispered and hung up.

Tia covered her eyes and let the gentle emotion pass. This was so unlike her. Crying at work. Because

Megan said she loved her. Although they weren't related by blood, Megan was the sister Tia never had. She vowed to look out for her more.

Glancing at the clock, she quickly clicked her computer mouse and went to eBay. She'd sold three more bags. She now had all the money she needed for an attorney. Congratulating herself, Tia exhaled. Her life was changing quickly. Ever since she'd let go of the revenge theory.

Hurriedly, she glanced at the clock and opened her e-mail.

Tonight's the night!

The plan was for Ginger to convince her husband that she was taking him to a five-acre lot and to make him believe she was onboard with his new lifestyle. Then she'd tell him that she was going to build them a house so he and his wives could live happily in Georgia. Once Ginger and her husband got to the newly razed lot, where there was no one for miles, the class would perform the intervention.

Before the night was over, they'd get Mr. Infidel Gary to sign the divorce papers. Then Ginger would be free.

That wasn't so bad, Tia thought. She scrolled down and gasped at the note left expressly for her.

Keep Byron busy until at least midnight. It's been confirmed that he's off work tonight. Don't let us down.

The sound of hurried steps made Tia close her e-mail and bring up her station's weather news.

She stood and stretched, walking around, getting a feel for the morning. Making love to Byron had been a treat she was glad she hadn't denied herself. He was all man, and being that close to him, so intimately, made her heart weak.

Heading back to her cubicle, she saw the crown of Vic's head. He searched frantically through his desk, then sat down, a bunch of papers strewn all over the desktop and floor.

Tia stopped. "Lose something?"

"More like somebody *took* something. It was right here." He started tearing up the desk again, then stopped. He looked crestfallen, and Tia didn't know what to do.

"Vic, is there some way I can help?"

"Give me back the money!"

"I wish I had money to give. I'm in the middle of some serious financial challenges—"

"Okay, whatever, Tia. We all know you've got issues. But let me just say, you're just wrong."

Vic stomped past her, leaving Tia outside his cube, alone. Looking around, she searched for someone who could explain what was going on. But it was still early, and most of the staff wouldn't start trickling in for another fifteen minutes.

Tia picked up the papers and put them in Vic's side drawer before going to her cubicle.

Honestly, he'd hurt her feelings, but she was going to keep that to herself. There was a logical explanation for his behavior, and eventually, he'd come and apologize.

Settling down to review the overnight weather updates, Tia was pulling data from the computer and fax machine when she turned around and ran into Alison.

Blond hair streamed down Alison's shoulders, and she enjoyed flicking it. She tossed her hair over one shoulder, then the other, and then back again.

Tia sighed. Alison looked like a horse. "Something I can do for you?"

"You're wanted in the break room," said Alison.

"Why? It's my turn to sit in on the Doppler enhancements meeting."

More hair tossing. "That can wait. This can't."

Alison threw out her hand for Tia to go ahead of her. Giving the woman a measuring look, Tia decided to go to the break room. This was obviously important.

She pushed the door open. All of the coworkers from her floor were standing around the room, looking uncomfortable. No one met her gaze. Not even Vic.

"What's going on?" Tia asked.

"Tia," Alison said, taking the role of leader, "money has gone missing in the office, and given that you've had some financial troubles, we thought you might want to say something to everyone."

Her first reaction was to tell Alison to put on a sturdier bra. But she didn't say that. She was going to stick to the subject. "I don't know what happened to anybody's money, but I noticed some change has disappeared from my desk, too. Does management know?"

"We were trying to spare you the embarrassment of management knowing about you 'borrowing,'" Alison said, using her fingers.

"What are you talking about?" Tia demanded. "I didn't take any money." She looked around at the disbelieving faces. "I didn't, and I don't appreciate the implication."

"Someone stole the candy money from Vic's desk, for his daughter's candy sale. He needs that back, Tia, and you were here late just about every day this week."

Tia's mouth fell open. "I was working," she explained to the crowded room. "This is ridiculous." Tia thought of every relaxation technique Fred had ever taught them. She breathed in and out, then smiled. "Vic, I'm sorry the money is gone, but I'm as much a victim as anyone else. Now if you'll excuse me, I have work to do."

"Just a minute, Tia." Another meteorologist, Faye, a woman Tia hardly ever spoke to, came forward. "For a long time, I've thought you've been given a bad rap. So I want to say publicly, I believe you. And, well, here."

She shoved five dollars into Tia's hand. "All those take-out bags in the refrigerator mean something. I've been down on my luck before, too. Keep your chin up. Things will get better," she said and left the room.

"Th-thank you, Faye," Tia said to the closing door. "But you don't have to do this. I'm just fine. I filed my taxes last night, and I'm getting a refund!"

Tia wanted to stop talking, but her coworkers had begun to file by her, many shoving money into her hands.

Alison looked as appalled as Tia felt. "We believe she's the one taking the money. Don't give it to her."

"Exactly," Tia said, in a way agreeing with Alison. "*I didn't take your money.* I don't need this. Thank you, but no, I can't. I've sold my purses online," she said to the late-night producer, Barb. Money began to fall onto the floor. "I'm getting an attorney, and I've cut off my home phone."

A knot wedged in Tia's throat. "You don't have to do this," she said to the maintenance man, Dickie. He'd shoved a five in her hand and took three ones back before leaving the room.

"Where's your car?" Ben asked. "You used to try to take the space closest to the stairs, and you know that's my favorite spot. I haven't had to battle with you lately. Where's your car?"

Tia eyed the dollars in her palms. "It was towed, and I haven't gotten it out yet. I need the attorney first."

Ben reached into his pocket and pulled out another twenty.

"No," Tia said, shoving all the money into his hands. "No! Please stop."

The remaining people in the break room stopped moving.

"Please, everyone, thank you for your thoughtfulness. But I'm going to be fine. I can't take your money. I don't need it. Really."

"But your car," Ben said.

"Has been delivered to the parking lot. Level three, row one."

Everyone in the room turned to put a face to the new male voice.

Tia knew it better than anyone. She'd heard it in every stage, from stressed to completely satisfied.

She looked over her shoulder and got her first full view of Byron in two days. She couldn't say how bad she'd missed him until now. "Hi," she murmured.

"Hi. Your car is downstairs," Byron said. "I just need you to sign off on some paperwork. Do you have a minute?"

He looked so official in his uniform. Shaved and pressed and authoritative and delicious.

Tia just wanted to jump into his arms and whisper "encore" in his ear.

Ben held the money, and Byron gave the entire scene an assessing look. "What's going on?" he asked.

"Nothing," Tia responded, holding up her hands. "A misunderstanding. Ben, please offer everyone their money back or give it to Vic for his daughter. Thank you."

"I—I don't know," he said, eyeing Byron, then Tia. "You look like you need to eat some real food. Here's my twenty. Happy birthday or something."

Tia wished the floor would open up and suck her into her next life.

"Okay. I appreciate it," she said.

Byron stepped inside the break room, holding the door as the rest of the staff members filed out.

Tia wiped her hands on her skirt, the twenty still in her palm. "Byron, I'll walk down with you."

They walked through the office, with everyone watching.

Bryon put his hand on the small of her back, and the women she passed smiled. At least they didn't think he was arresting her.

Inside the elevator they stood side by side. Until the doors closed.

Then Tia was in his arms, and Byron lifted her practically off her feet.

Their mouths met in an urgent embrace that expressed need and desire. "I missed you," she whispered when he pressed his mouth up and down her neck.

"Likewise," he groaned, no longer official. Just Byron.

Tia liked him this way. She could love him, she knew.

"What floor are we on?" she asked.

"Three." He kissed her mouth. "Two," he said and let his hands explore, and when his eyes widened in surprise, she just grinned.

When the elevator opened, the people waiting to board had no idea he'd just fingered her in the elevator.

Standing by her car, Tia couldn't stop her body from humming. "You're coming by tonight. Megan's going to come home tomorrow."

"I can't," he said, squinting into the sun.

"Can you take those things off? I can't see your eyes."

Byron lifted his glasses. "Better, Ms. Bossy?"

"Yes." Tia looked at her little blue Honda. "I can't believe I missed her so much. How'd you get her here?"

"The wrecker."

"How much is it?"

"Nothing, ma'am."

Tia glanced over her shoulder and saw why he'd ma'amed her. Chance was glaring at them. Tia turned back to Byron, hoping maybe a bird would fall from the sky and take Chance out. One could hope.

"Why is it nothing?" Tia asked Byron. "Is this wrecker fee amnesty day?"

"No, smarty. There was a little convincing from law enforcement to return the vehicle to the rightful owner since it had been towed illegally."

"You stood up for me?"

"Don't get all gooey-eyed. It was a collaborative effort between my department and the wrecker company. He's statewide and had some tickets he needed a little more time to pay. Several departments came together and made a deal."

"You stood up for me. I guess you think you're going to be thanked big time, huh?"

He grinned down at her, and her legs turned to mush. "Affirmative. Your boss is still standing there. What is her deal?"

"She's just weird. Stop looking. Any minute a bird is going to poop on her head. That would really make my day."

They both laughed.

"Sign here, please," Byron said. "Do you have your keys?"

"There's one in the glove compartment." Tia tried the locked door. "Do you have one of those thingies?"

Byron rested his hands on his belt. "Another day we're going to have a serious talk about why you should never leave a key to the car *in* the car."

He walked to his trunk, got the instrument, and opened the door. Reaching inside, he got the key and put it in her hand.

"Is your boss still there?" he asked.

"No, she's gone. Probably planning how she's going to write me up again."

"That sounds too stressful. I'd seriously consider looking for another job."

"I could give you that same advice. You should try and not be so good all the time. Might change your perspective about life."

"My perspective is just fine, thanks."

"I'm just suggesting you might not be so boring."
He moved very slowly and stared at her.

Tia slapped her hand over her mouth. "I just
mean that you might have more fun." She giggled.
"Never mind. I will say that since all this has happened to me, I have a greater appreciation for
others. I'm just suggesting you might, too."

"I like people just fine, and my job is great,"
Byron informed her. "After tomorrow, my life will
be exceptional."

"What happens then?"

"Anger management class will be over, and I'll
get my promotion to detective."

A lump formed in Tia's throat. His life *was* fine.
"Detective? Wow. That's quite a leap. Congratulations."

Before she could think twice, she hugged him
and stepped back. Byron had to finish the class and
so did she. And they had to do it without getting
into trouble. Being together tonight was best for
both of them.

"Did you like my elevator surprise?" she said, suddenly kittenish. She had to convince him to come
spend the night with her.

They stood side by side, and Tia could see his re-
flection in the window of her car.

"The thong? Hell yeah. That was a sexy, sweet
surprise. You've messed up my head for the rest of
the day."

Tia grinned. "There's more where that came from."

"Can I handle it?" he asked.

She chanced a look at him. "You've done a stellar
job so far. I'll bring the Italian food. You bring the
wine. Seven o'clock okay?"

"I'm off tonight, so seven is good."

"I know. Bring the handcuffs, and I get to wear the shades."

Tia walked back to the building, and before entering the revolving door, she looked over her shoulder and gave him a glimpse of what he'd be getting.

His head fell back, and she smiled all the way to her desk.

At her desk, Tia dialed Rusty, the attorney, and held her breath while she completed a wire transfer of money from her account to his. Within ten minutes, he called her back.

"Tia Amberson," she answered.

"Young lady. Your hearing with Judge Dunn is Monday morning at nine, his chambers."

She blinked in surprise. "You're amazing. I've been leaving messages with his office for a week."

Rusty laughed. "Helps that I've been around the block long enough to have known a lot of these judges before they became judges. Mutual respect. Fax over that lease agreement and let me have a look-see. I'll see you at eight-thirty Monday at the courthouse, in the lobby."

"Thank you, Rusty." She wanted to say more but knew she'd said enough. "Thank you."

"You're welcome. Be good this weekend."

"Yes, sir. Good-bye."

Chapter Twenty-one

Stressed beyond belief, Tia stepped onto the elevator at 4:30 p.m., and tears welled in her eyes. The pressure of the job had finally gotten the best of her. Although she'd declined the money, many of her coworkers still believed that she was stealing from them.

If they only knew what she'd been through to try to get her life back on track, they would know she was a woman of integrity.

Tears slid down her face, and she brushed them away as the doors opened and Ronnie/Rhonda boarded with his mail cart.

"Hey, Peacock," he said happily, until he looked closely at her. "What's with the tears?"

Tia went into his waiting arms and burst out crying.

"I didn't steal from anyone. I've done everything I can to get my life back on track. I spilled my guts to the entire office, telling them everything," she rattled on. "I know they think I'm a basket case. Then they were trying to give me money. I turned it down, but they still think I'm a thief. Your sister is treating me like I'm from an alien nation, and it's too much. I can't do this anymore."

Tia threw up her hands. I was hired to be a meteorologist, not a glorified flunky. No offense to anyone who might have a low-paying, low-respect job." She leaned back to see how he was dressed. "Ronnie. I'm just tired of the nonsense, and I'm hungry." The tears kept falling as she fumbled inside her purse. "And the old Tia would have had tissue in her purse."

Pitifully, Tia cried harder.

Rhonda/Ronnie gave her his hanky, and she opened her mouth to continue her rant, but the bell rang, and the doors opened for new passengers. Tia turned away from them. She didn't feel like being the brunt of any further office gossip.

After the other passengers exited, Rhonda/Ronnie guided Tia off at the fifth floor and took her to a small office.

"Calm down, Peacock. Let's figure this out together."

"I'm quitting, Ronnie. I can't do this job anymore. The mental struggle is off the chain. And, for the record, I've never said cunnilinglus on the air, so explain to me how Alison is a better choice than me for second chair?" Tia demanded. "I don't think so."

"You are the better choice. The best," Rhonda/Ronnie assured her, "but if you quit, what are you going to do?"

One tear after another streaked her cheeks. "I don't know. I can't really think right now. I need some space. I need for all of this to be over."

"You are right about that." Rhonda/Ronnie rummaged through a file cabinet, pulled out a piece of paper, and handed it to her.

"You have a doctor's appointment, and that requires you to have the whole day off. This way you can think things through and still have a job."

Despite knowing in her heart that she wanted to quit, Tia saw the practicality in Rhonda/Ronnie's thinking. She caught him in a tight hug. "You're a great friend."

"Thank you. Tia?"

"Yes?"

"Remember when you told me about the woman who slapped Chance? What did she look like?"

"She was white, severe hairstyle. In fact, everything about her was severe. Dark hair, dark clothes. Sour look on her face. She looked like she meant business. Like someone you didn't want to cross."

Rhonda/Ronnie inhaled sharply but didn't comment further.

Tia didn't care. The nonsense that had nothing to do with work had finally broken her.

Chance had won.

Tia would tender her resignation tomorrow.

Rhonda/Ronnie pressed a kiss to Tia's forehead. "Go home and chill. Call me tomorrow if you're not going to come in."

"OK."

Tia thought about what she was going to do with her life as she drove toward Megan's.

She was immeasurably glad to be in her own car again. Taking the bus had been fine, but there was nothing like her car, her music, and her privacy.

Tia had to admit, though, that part of her tension

was due to the fact that anger management class was ending tomorrow.

And she was frustrated about work, stressed about her appointment Monday with the judge, and anxious to get on with her life.

She fished her cell phone out of her purse and wanted to call Byron and tell him to come over now, but if they got into the hot and heavy business of lovemaking, he might not want to stay later tonight. And she needed to help the ladies; she'd promised.

Pulling up in front of Megan's, she noticed Kirk's car and Megan getting out.

"Hey, you." Tia ran over and hugged her friend. Megan had parted her hair in the front and combed the short strands over to the side. The ends flipped up. She hadn't bothered with make-up, letting just a hint of gloss outline her tentative smile.

She looked beautiful.

The vacant look of pain and hurt was gone from her dark brown eyes, although she now had trouble meeting Tia's.

"You look great," Tia told her softly.

"For someone that's crazy, right?" Low self-esteem swirled around her friend, and for a moment Tia felt sorry for Megan. But the feeling washed away as the sun burst through the clouds.

For a few seconds, they all shielded their eyes, watching Mother Nature show off.

"You're not crazy." Tia held Megan's cheeks. "You're a little to the left, just like me and Kirk. We've been waiting for you to join us. Now you're finally normal."

Megan laughed then, sounding like her old self for a few seconds. "Thank you," she whispered. "I needed that."

Regaining the strength in her voice, she looked at the town house. "I didn't mean to drop all the responsibility of my renovations into your lap."

"It wasn't a bother at all," Tia reassured her. "They did most of the work while I was at work. Get this. The foreman leaves a note about what to touch and what not to."

"Wow. That is nice," Megan said.

Kirk came around from the trunk, a handsome smile on his face. Tia gave Megan the eye. Kirk was one good-looking man.

"Um, Kirk," Megan said, suddenly shy. "Would you like to come in? I don't know the condition of the house, but you're welcome to visit for a little while."

"Sure," he said, and Tia saw it. Love glimmered in his eyes.

How was that possible? He had only seen Megan a few times before today. And it hadn't been under the best of circumstances. But Kirk was a rescuer, and when Megan needed to be rescued, he'd stepped up, and now he seemed to want to stick around.

Tia's first instinct was to offer them advice, but she didn't. Just a couple of months ago she, Megan, and Rachel had sat inside, berating their love lives and talking revenge, and look where that had gotten them.

Rachel was no longer Tia's friend, and Megan had just come from a short stay at a mental institution.

Tia could recount every upheaval in her life of the last few months and swallowed any words of caution she might have wanted to offer, because the only time her life made sense was when she and Byron were together.

Walking up the stairs behind the couple, Tia realized that their presence would ruin her evening, and she didn't have a plan B. She turned and started down the stairs.

"Tia, why are you home so early?"

In that instant, Tia decided not to heap any more of her problems on Megan. They were both healing and would have to do some of it on their own. "I just needed to get out of work a little early."

"What happened?" Kirk asked, not buying that story.

Tia shook her head. "Nothing important."

"I hope you still have a job," Megan said. "You need health insurance. The APC wasn't a country club, but they charged country club prices. I'd have been better off going to Hawaii."

"Another career is just a phone call away, Tia. You have choices," Kirk said, and Megan touched his arm.

"We all do. I learned that," Megan said. "Tia, are you coming inside?"

"I-I need to take care of something. You don't need me right this second, do you?"

Kirk looked at Megan and shook his head.

"I guess not," Megan said, opening the door. "Should I expect you back?"

"Definitely. But maybe not tonight, unless you absolutely need me. Hey, do you have my extra car key? I'd feel more secure having more than two."

Megan handed over the key without question. "Tia, I'm going to be fine. Is it the cop?" she asked, digging a little.

She couldn't contain her smile. "Yes."

Tia realized she missed this part of her relationship with Megan and Rachel. They used to share their lives, their pain, talk about their men, and it was like having sisters.

After all she'd been through, Tia wondered if she and Rachel could be friends again. All she could do was try.

Sometime soon Tia vowed to call and apologize.

"Megan, he's something else," Tia said, knowing there wasn't another phrase that said it better.

A smile lifted Tia's mood right off the ground. The joy of being with Byron filled her with energy.

"Goodness, you're practically glowing. We have a lot to talk about, but not now. Have fun," Megan said and winked.

Tia hopped into her car, raced to the ATM, and withdrew a hundred dollars.

She rationalized that in order to fulfill her obligation to the class, she'd need working capital. After she'd bought all the necessities, Tia called Byron. "Where are you?"

"On my way to your place," he answered. "Traffic on 285 isn't too bad, so I should be there in about twenty minutes. I thought you'd be there by now." his voice dipped low enough to make her thighs tingle. "Waiting. Preferably undressed."

Tia giggled seductively. "I was, but Megan came home today."

"She's there? Right now?"

"Yep." Tia sympathized with his groan of frustration. "I have a plan B, and a plan C, based upon what you might like."

"OK," Byron said cautiously. "What's your plan B?"

"I'm about a mile from the Eight-eighty Motel. We can get a room and have a great time, although it's a bit seedy, or plan C is we can spend the evening in my car. I know it's not big enough, but if we recline both the seats, you'd only have to leave your legs hanging out the window. The other important parts would be inside, with me."

"So you just want me for my—"

A horn blew loud and long. "Talk about great timing," Tia said after they stopped laughing.

"I have a suggestion, not that yours weren't good."

"I'm open to good ideas," she said.

"We can go to my place," Byron offered.

Tia's heart thundered. This was a leap for him, a major step in the relationship, and one she hadn't been expecting. They'd gone through a lot together, and Tia was glad to know that her feelings for him weren't one-sided.

She pulled into the parking lot of a Walgreen's to organize her thoughts.

"Tia?" said Bryon.

"I was just deciding if I wanted to go to your place."

A long moment of silence passed between them. "What's your decision?" Bryon asked.

"Tell me where to go."

Tia followed the directions right to Byron's front door and parked on his driveway.

They got out of their cars at the same time.

She drank in the sight of him.

Dark denim jeans and a white long-sleeved mock T-shirt covered him, and all she could think about was how much she wanted him to be undressed.

Tia pulled the bag of food from the car, along with a pink glossy bag from the lingerie store. He had bags in his hands, too.

Byron lived on a quiet street where the houses were spaced a good distance from each other. Peace emanated from the picturesque environment, and Tia was aware of how much someone like him, in his line of work, needed peace. She was glad to be in his world.

His keys tinkled as he unlocked the front door, and a gentle breeze billowed around the porch and kissed her cheek.

Tia smiled and looked up. Byron was looking straight at her. She stepped into the house after him, and he took the bag of food. "Hungry?" he asked.

"No."

"Thirsty?"

"No."

The strap to her purse slid down her arm, and she put the lingerie bag and her jacket on the kitchen chair. Byron smiled, and his dimple winked.

He backed up slowly as she advanced.

"Do you want anything?" he asked.

Tia already felt like she was coming apart. "Just you."

"I'm yours."

Tia didn't feel elegant or flirty or even sexy. She felt like a woman with power that couldn't be quantified.

In an instant, she was in his arms. Their bodies were as close as they could be, clothed. Byron remedied that by taking his off first. This was the second time she'd gotten to admire him as he stripped, unashamed of his nakedness.

When she began to take off her clothes, he knelt down, and on every uncovered body part, he placed lingering kisses. By the time Tia had gotten to her thong, she was nearly ready to climax, and he hadn't even touched her there.

She tried to pleasure him, but Byron was on a mission, and Tia was his subject. When his tongue finally did meet her G-spot, orgasms racked her body. Even hours later, his appetite for making love was insatiable.

Tia vowed to herself that she'd keep up with him, and when she was sure he'd had enough, she fell asleep in his arms.

Hours later Tia awoke to the strains of Najee, but no Byron. She found one of his shirts and pulled it on as she walked from room to room, admiring the beautiful pieces of bronze art that graced the shelves and glass tables.

His furniture was dark, but what caught Tia's eye was the artwork. There were vases and masks, African statues, and interesting framed tapestries.

His taste was exquisite.

"Byron?" she called and heard nothing. She retraced her steps and ended up at the front door. Peeking out, Tia saw her car, but not his.

She thought maybe he'd gone to the store.

Suddenly hungry, Tia looked for the food they'd forgotten about and found it in the refrigerator. She pulled it out and was about to heat it up when she saw the wine, a corkscrew, and a note.

Her heart tripped as she looked at his bold scrawl. Yet dread flowed over her like one of the dazzling climaxes Byron had elicited from her earlier.

> *Tia,*
> *I've gone to stop A M group from getting into trouble. Please stay home. I'll be back soon, and we can resume where we left off. Love, Byron.*

Tia's mouth fell open. She reread the note. Five times.

She quickly dialed his cell phone. "Where are you, Byron?"

"Stay in bed," he ordered her.

"That's very sexist and domineering and bossy."

"If I thought you'd listen, I'd say it nicer. But for the sake of giving you the benefit of the doubt, I'll say it differently. Please stay home and wait for me."

Tia ignored her hunger pangs and scurried into the bedroom to get dressed. "I'm a reporter."

"A meteorologist," he countered. "You're not on the night beat. You report the weather. You can stay home and let me handle this, and everything will be fine."

Tia thought of the promise she'd made to her anger management classmates. Along the way, she'd let Rachel down, and that's why they weren't friends anymore. Tia didn't want to shortchange another person she called friend.

"Byron, I can't. I have to see this through. If you hadn't left me, we could have done this together."

"When are you going to grow up?" he asked, sounding exasperated. "I'm a cop, Tia, and this isn't a game. Someone could get hurt."

"I know. That's why I have to be there. To be the voice of reason. Nothing bad will happen if I'm there."

"Baby," he said, "you don't have the power to predict the future."

"You don't either, Byron. We're both taking a chance."

"But I have a gun, and I'm authorized to use it."

Just the thought of there being a shooting made Tia cringe.

"Nothing that serious will happen," she said, slipping her feet into her shoes.

"You can't leave," he told her as she hurried to her car, her purse over her shoulder.

"I'm already outside."

"I have your car keys," Byron said, sounding grim.

Tia stopped, momentarily stunned. "You really big sneak! Okay," she said, palming the backup metal key. "You win. I'll be here when you get back. Your phone's ringing. I'd better go. Camilla Ryan. I'll let that roll over to your voice mail, okay?"

"That's my sister. Tell her I'm on an errand and will call her tomorrow. I'll see you in a little bit."

"Okay," she said, hanging up.

Tia hurried back to the front door to put the phone inside.

"Hello?"

"Oh. Hello. Is Byron there?"

"No. May I take a message?"

"Who is this?"

"Tia Amberson, a friend of Byron's, Camilla. I'm sorry, we haven't met, but I saw your name on the caller ID, and I was on the phone with your brother, and he said you were his sister." Tia took a

big breath. "Sorry for going on and on. Is there a
message I can give him?"

"Just tell him I said thank you for the Prada,
Gucci, and Coach purses, but I can't take any more.
My husband is beginning to think Byron is buying
them hot or something."

Tia couldn't speak. "Do you have the green Baby
Phat?"

"Girrrl, that's my favorite! How'd you know? Oh
boy. I don't think we're supposed to be talking."

"He's been buying my purses off eBay," Tia whispered. "How many?" she asked Camilla.

"Thirteen."

"Oh my goodness." Tia covered her mouth, cal-
culating the hefty total of all the purses. She'd
hired an attorney with that money.

Love, Byron.

His handsome handwriting wove through her mind
and down into her chest. Tia knew she had to hurry.

"I think my brother has some very strong feelings
for you."

"I do, too. Camilla, do you mind if I hang up
now? I need to go and . . . get him."

"Please do, sister."

The words wrapped Tia's heart just a little tighter.
If she survived this night, she and Byron had some
serious talking to do. "Bye, Camilla."

Byron's phone began to ring as she put it in the
house. She saw that it was him but didn't stop to
answer it. She had a promise to fulfill.

Chapter Twenty-two

Byron trudged over the last rise in the Georgia clay, moving quickly toward the screaming. A group of women crowded around a fire, a seated figure in the center.

He was screaming.

Byron approached with extreme caution.

The women had champagne flutes in their hands, drinking and chatting as if the man weren't there.

Ginger was dressed in a black leather dress, a long skirt fanned out like a cape around her legs. She giggled with the other women and, for the first time, seemed tapped in to the real world.

"Oh no! Officer Official is here. He's here to ruin our fun. How'd you know we were here?" Peggy asked, staring at Byron.

"I've got my sources."

"Tia ratted us out! I can't believe her," Ann Marie said from the crowd that had assembled behind Pebbles.

"Tia didn't tell me anything," Byron said calmly, as he put himself between the man and the women.

The ladies didn't know he'd been shadowing them online for quite some time, waiting for them to disclose the time and date of their revenge. Once he found out, he planned every move—up until now. Having Tia at his house, immobilized, was like icing on the cake.

They'd gotten Gary good. His chest bare, he smelled sickly sweet. He'd been tied to the chair, his legs wrapped in heavy duct tape, his arms and chest bound around the top of the chair. A tie had been used as a blindfold, so he couldn't see.

"Tia wouldn't do that," Pebbles agreed. "But I wouldn't put it past him to have read her e-mails."

"I *did* read the e-mails, but not because Tia let me." Byron cleared his throat. "She did exactly what you all asked her to do, and that was to keep me occupied."

"She couldn't be that great if you're here," Betty said.

"That's not nice," Ginger said, frowning.

"My accomplice was Fred," Byron said.

The scared man emerged from the darkness, shaking in his shiny new tennis shoes. "Ladies, don't hate me. I thought you all were going to commit a crime. I'm duty-bound to notify the authorities if that happens. I was the antagonizing voice in the e-mails."

"That was you, Fred?" Ginger asked, smiling.

"Y-yes." He tried so hard not to stammer. Byron was proud of him.

"You did a good job of scaring everybody."

Ginger's compliment seemed to make Fred stand taller. "Right, girls? Byron?"

The other women in the class nodded their heads.

Buoyed by their support, Fred pulled a folder from beneath his jacket. "The good news is that you all didn't do anything against the law. The even better news is . . ." Fred hesitated, and Byron thought the FAMU marching band was going to stomp out. Fred smiled like he'd been skewered. "You all passed the class!"

Cheers went up, and the women linked arms and danced around the fire. More champagne was poured, and Peggy even gave Byron a plastic champagne flute. "Yours is ginger ale, like mine." She lifted her flute and walked away.

"Will someone pay attention to me?" Gary whined.

"Shut up, Gary!" Ginger ran from her circle of friends and squeezed his jaw until all they could hear was a high-pitched squeal.

"You came here because you thought you were going to have sex with me and other women. As far as I'm concerned, you're lucky to have both your balls. You keep talking, and we can change that."

The entire group watched in stunned silence as the usually timid woman dragged her nails lightly around Gary's chest, shoulders, and back.

He bounced and groaned as if his seat were getting hot. "More, more," he whined.

"You two are sick," Pebbles said, disgusted.

Ginger stopped, took a deep breath, and exhaled audibly. "Not really. You'll see."

"What are you going to do to us? Are we under arrest?" Pebbles asked Byron.

All of the women stared at Bryon with wide, scared eyes.

The law dictated that he take them in and, at a minimum, get statements.

But after all they'd been through, Byron would use his better judgment.

"Congratulations, ladies," he said quietly. "Go home. The night is over."

Despite his last instructions, they rushed him, covering him with grateful hugs. Byron bent down and accepted each one.

"Ow. Ow!" Gary complained. "Can somebody scratch me? These bugs are eating me alive."

Ginger and the rest of the ladies turned and took one last look at Gary. Mosquitoes covered him, feeding on his blood.

"See. I told you," Ginger whispered to the group.

"You're not crazy," Pebbles responded as they started toward the hill. "You're certifiable."

"And rich," Ginger laughed. "Good riddance, Gary."

Byron waited until the last car had pulled off before he looked at Gary Kelston.

"Officer, are you still here?"

"Yes, Mr. Kelston. I'm still here."

"Untie me, you nimrod. That bitch isn't going to get away with this. I'm going to blow every one of them to bits." This guy was a first-class jerk.

"Sir, calling me names isn't going to get you out of here any faster. In fact, after you get medical assistance, you'll be arrested and booked."

Byron dialed his cell phone and gave their location as Gary shouted obscenities.

"Arrested for what?" he demanded when Byron wouldn't take the bait of his anger.

"Making terroristic threats."

"I didn't do any such thing! You're one of them, sissy boy. The only man in their class," he shouted derisively. "They should've slapped a skirt on you and called you Sally. Get these bugs off of me!"

Byron looked into the cloudless sky. The rain had passed, leaving the air clear and fresh. Byron lifted his cell phone. "Cancel the EMTs," he said.

"What the hell are you doing?"

Byron snapped the phone closed. "You want to insult me, Kelston? Then your help goes right out the window. Good night. I'll pick up what the bugs leave tomorrow."

"No! No! You can't leave me here. I have a right to your help. Just like I have a right to teach my wife who's boss."

"My jurisdiction ended twenty yards ago, at the top of this dirt hill," said Byron.

"I'm sorry, okay? Damn. You act as if I'm not a civilian in distress. She thinks that document she made me sign is valid, but I did it under duress. Therefore, I'm still entitled to her money."

"You have the right to remain silent. Anything you say can and will be used against you in a court of law. You have the right . . ."

"I'm not under arrest. Why are you reading me my rights?" Gary said, wiggling and bouncing in his chair.

"As I said, anything you say could be used against you in a court of law."

"To hell with that. I didn't create this situation, but I'm damn sure going to finish it. Ah! Ah!

Ahhh!" Gary yelped as bugs devoured him. As Byron struggled to see what more was happening, he realized Gary didn't have any bottoms on, and his privates had been smeared with honey and whipped cream. It was like a mosquito convention was in town.

Byron gave the women ten points for originality. The rescue squad from Ladder Company 15 arrived, along with the paramedics and a police squad car.

This was going to be funny for a long time.

"I need to scratch. I need to scratch," Gary blubbered. "Please scratch me."

Byron just shook his head. This was hilarious.

"The rescue squad is on its way down. It'll be just a minute more."

"Please scratch my nipples. I beg of you," Gary whined.

"Dude, you'd be better off asking God to kill you. Now, you should be quiet before they get into your mouth."

Gary's mouth clamped closed just as a commotion ensued behind Byron.

Byron hoped and prayed it wasn't what he thought, but when he turned around, all he could do was shake his head.

An officer had Tia by the arm and was escorting her through the damp earth toward him.

Byron stepped back as the paramedics had a good laugh. One even took a picture before they began to attend to Gary.

"Officer Rivers, do you know this woman?" the uniformed cop asked.

"No, he doesn't," Tia answered.

"Yes, she's my—"

"I'm a reporter, and I'm covering a story," Tia answered.

"She's my girlfriend," said Byron.

"You do or don't know him?" the officer asked Tia.

"I do know Byron."

"In that case, you both need to come down to the station, make a statement, and be questioned by the captain before this is a done deal. Do you know the victim?" the officer asked Tia.

Byron looked at Tia, sending her a silent warning, but she seemed hell-bent on doing things her way.

"Indirectly," Tia answered.

Gary was being driven by on a stretcher and saw Tia. "She's one of those angry women who did this to me. I want her arrested."

Tia put her hands behind her back. She knew the drill.

"I have the right to remain silent . . ." she began.

Byron snagged her arm. "She was at my house, in my bed. And that's where she's going. I'll make all the statements that need to be made. Tia, let's go."

Byron escorted Tia to her car, then gave her the key to his house. "The way I left you is the way I hope you'll be when I get home."

She looked up and smiled at him. "Definitely, with one addition."

Byron leaned his forearms on the roof. "What's that?"

"I'm going to pick up some honey."

He rapped on the roof of the car with his knuckles. That was a hell of a good idea. "Affirmative. See you in a couple hours."

Chapter Twenty-three

Judge Dunn looked at Tia and smiled. "I knew we'd meet again. I see that your ex continues to be a thorn in your side. I understand that he rented out the house before my ruling. Why wasn't this brought to me sooner?"

Judge Dunn looked at the various officials in his chambers, and no one replied. Byron and another deputy stood in the back of the room, while the clerk taking dictation sat off to the side.

Tia and Rusty sat facing the judge's desk.

"This is ridiculous," Judge Dunn exclaimed after reading pages of documents Tia had submitted, proving ownership of the condo. "Where have you been living?"

"With . . . people. Friends," Tia answered. "I had to sell some personal property to raise the money to get an attorney, who got me an appointment for today."

"Why didn't you call my office?"

"I did. I was told it would take months to get on your calendar. I didn't know what else to do. I went to the condo with Officer Rivers, but when we were presented with the lease, I was told I'd have to wait for a new ruling from you."

Judge Dunn stared down Rusty Cavitt. "How much are appointments going for with you, Rusty?"

"That ain't why we're here, Judge Dunn."

"How much did you charge Ms. Amberson?"

"Seventy-five hundred dollars. I was led to believe there were extenuating circumstances."

The judge whistled. "That would make you the most expensive attorney in the world, right? Georgia sure is blessed that you decided to open your office here in our fair state, with your correspondence law degree, huh, Rusty?"

Tia glared at her attorney. "You never told me that."

"You never asked, Ms. Amberson," Rusty drawled back.

"How much is an hour of your time, Mr. Cavitt?" Tia asked.

Rusty shifted uncomfortably in his chair. "One hundred seventy-five dollars."

Tia glanced at her watch, then at the judge. "We've got four minutes. Then I'm in for three hundred fifty dollars. Can we make this snappy?"

"You betcha," said Judge Dunn.

"When can she get her house back, Judge?" Rusty asked.

"Today."

Tia wanted to spring from her seat, but she held on to her skirt as the judge gave Rusty a down-the-nose glare.

"The tenant is ordered to vacate immediately. Her property is to be put in a truck, and she can drive it to the destination of her choice within fifty miles of Atlanta. Notify the sheriff of this emergency eviction. Officer Delta, you are hereby assigned to make sure Ms. Amberson gets into her home. Officer Rivers, you are dismissed from this case."

The judge stacked the papers, shaking his head, then continued.

"Let me say that this is a troubling travesty of justice. You all have failed Ms. Amberson, from members of my staff, who I will personally deal with, to you, Officer Rivers."

"Sir, with all due respect, I tried to reach you, and you were out of town," said Byron.

"Then you should have camped out on my doorstep until you got me and until the directive I'd given you weeks ago had been fulfilled. She has been homeless, arrested, shamed, and from the looks of things, nearly fired. Then she has to sell property to hire a price-gouging attorney. Ridiculous! I have failed you, too, Ms. Amberson, and on behalf of this entire justice system, I extend my heartfelt apology. Is there anything else I can do for you, Ms. Amberson?"

"No, sir." The lump in Tia's throat made it impossible for her to speak.

"Ms. Amberson, I want verbal confirmation to this number, my cell phone, when you have been installed in your home. Officer Rivers, I want verbal confirmation from you that the locks at Ms. Amberson's premises have been changed, at the police department's expense, and that you have driven out of this young woman's life." The judge handed a card to Byron. "Officer Delta, you are to notify me if the slightest order isn't followed. Clear?" he asked the severe-looking officer.

"Yes, sir!"

"Rusty, dig out your checkbook," Judge Dunn continued. "You are refunding this young lady all but one hundred seventy-five dollars of her money, or I will not support your fund-raiser for aging cowboys."

"That's extortion!" Rusty complained.

"Theft by manipulation is what I call it," Judge Dunn answered. "Ms. Amberson, do you have anything else for Mr. Cavitt?"

"No, sir."

"Then it would behoove you to fire him now."

Tia looked her attorney in the eye. "You're fired."

"Anything for anyone else in this room?" the judge asked. Tia didn't look at Byron. He could have done more, and he hadn't. He'd wanted to play rescuer, and she'd fallen right into his trap by needing so badly to be rescued. She'd learned to stand on her own two feet. And for the first time since her breakup with Dante, she'd be standing alone.

"No," Tia said. "Nothing."

"Officer Delta, please escort Ms. Amberson home."

Chapter Twenty-four

Tia walked into work, feeling lighter than she'd felt in months. She'd been in her condo for two days, and in that length of time, she grown to love the place.

It needed painting and other cosmetic fixes, but she was finally there. In her own home.

She pushed the empty brown box under her arm, trying not to think about the twenty-five resumes she'd sent out this morning.

Mixed emotions about quitting her job warred inside of her, but after all the thought and reminiscing, the conclusion remained the same. This was the right thing to do.

Tia's coworkers had begun to trickle in, but she ignored them as she stood outside her cubicle looking in.

Five years of her life had been spent in this little box. She'd seen new people come and go, bright and talented people move up and onward. Now it was her turn.

"I see you've decided to grace us with your

presence. How bold of you," Chance said from behind Tia.

Calm for the first time since she'd been put on the action plan, Tia turned to her boss.

"You're a tyrant with a God complex. An evil little person who let power go to her head, except you're powerless over me. All you've done is harass, antagonize, and treat me unfairly. And I want you to know, I don't have to take it anymore. I'm filing a lawsuit against you. I'm tired of being your bitch. Now if you will excuse me, I'm taking the rest of my earned vacation."

"All vacation has to be approved by me at least two weeks in advance. If you leave, I will consider it desertion of your job. Thank you," Chance said, with an elated smile. "You still aren't bright. You were almost home free, and then I'd have had to pick on someone else. *Idiot*," she said under her breath.

No, she didn't call me an idiot. Before Tia could think twice, she shoved Chance in the back, sending her flying onto the carpet. People poured out of their cubes at her screams.

Chance struggled to get up as change poured from her pockets. Looking horrified, she scrambled to pick up the coins. She stopped at shiny black shoes.

"Chance, what are you doing?" her father asked.

"Firing Tia. She just assaulted me. Call 911."

Nobody moved. Tia held her breath as the Normans made their way down to where she stood.

"Sweetheart, are you okay?" Mrs. Norman asked.

"I'm fine," Tia said, wiping hair from her eyes. She realized then that she was crying. She turned around and continued throwing things into her nearly full box. "I've just had it. The pressure is too much. Thank you, Mr. Norman. Mrs. Norman, I appreciate everything you've done, but I quit."

"Good, you were fired, anyway," Chance sniped.

"Wait," Mrs. Norman said, waving her hands to calm everyone down. "Winton and I have something to say. We've heard rumors about people's belongings going missing. We have received written complaints and anonymous phone calls about the unhappiness of the staff because someone has been stealing from them.

"Well, Winton and I aren't ones to turn our backs on situations, so we had some security cameras installed. I'm sorry to say that we know who the culprit is."

"Tia," Alison said loud and clear. "I'll call her boyfriend. He'll have to do his duty as a cop and arrest her. I'll also notify the news crew so they can get a shot of her handcuffed. It looks good if we can 'out' one of our own."

"Alison, *you're* fired," Mrs. Norman said, looking disgusted. "People are going to think you were sexually abused, the way you keep saying that C word for cumulus on TV. Every time I hear it, I swear, all of my blood vessels want to burst."

"It's me, Mrs. Norman, *Alison*." She dragged out her own name. "I didn't do anything wrong. That's Tia. She's the screwup."

"Somebody, please get her away from me," said Mrs. Norman.

Two of the male interns urged Alison toward the elevator, put her inside, and made sure the door was closed before returning to the action.

"Mrs. Norman, I didn't steal the money, but this is exactly what I was talking about," Tia interjected. "This isn't a professional work environment anymore. I've worked my butt off for this station, and all Chance can remember is the one time I, in the heat of passion, made one big mistake."

Tia threw up her hands. "I know how to take responsibility for my actions. What I did was wrong, but this is more wrong."

"Like you would know," Chance muttered, tapping her foot impatiently.

"Enough." Mr. Norman stepped forward. "Chance, do you want to tell your coworkers anything?"

"They're not my coworkers. They're my employees."

"Last opportunity, darling," Mrs. Norman urged her daughter.

Tia wondered what was going on but decided against getting involved in anyone else's junk. Her business was in the cubicle, and she decided to hurry things along.

She had another call to make.

"I have done nothing wrong," Chance snorted. "I can spot-check desks."

"Occasionally, yes, but you stole from them," Mr. Norman said. "Even this morning." The elevator opened, but all eyes were on the screens stationed around the room. The digital picture showed Chance going from one office to another, helping herself to whatever she could find. In one week, not only had she stolen money, but she'd eaten three of Vic's candy bars.

"This had been going on for about four months, and it's time it stopped," Mr. Norman said in a resigned tone.

Angry glares were directed at Chance, who looked uncomfortable now that she was busted.

"I wasn't stealing. I borrowed a quarter. Who's going to miss twenty-five cents? You're that stingy?" Chance said to the angry faces that stared at her. "You're all cheap. Fine. I'm sorry. Now get back to work. Everybody except Tia. She's leaving."

"Don't speak to her like that again."

Rhonda/Ronnie walked from the direction of the stairwell, and Tia couldn't help but wonder what was next. Her mouth fell open.

Gone were his tight leather pants and pink shirt. He'd exchanged them for a black Hugo Boss suit and tie. He came and stood beside Tia. "Chance, you're fired."

"Please," Chance snorted in disbelief. "You can't fire me. I'm the boss."

"Not anymore. We had a meeting, and two-thirds agree. We love you, and we know you're gambling again."

"Ronnie," Tia said. "Don't."

"I'm sorry, sweetie, but my sister was about to destroy this company. We have to confront this. Chance, if you want help, we'll help you fight this gambling addiction. That's why you've been stealing money. That's why you tried to fire Tia. You wanted to replace her with your bookie's niece. Then you wouldn't have had to pay any more money. But Tia didn't leave like a good girl."

"Ronnie, what are you doing?" Chance asked, her voice pleading, as her gaze darted around the room. "Tia is a terrible weatherwoman. She doesn't have the look that people want to see."

"If you think all they want to see is someone that's dumb and blond, you don't give the public much credit, but that's okay. I've got better things to do with my life than waste it here," Tia retorted. The smattering of applause left her feeling not so lonely. She started for the elevator, saying good-bye to the few people who were brave enough to apologize. With each step, she felt better.

Ronnie caught up to her and stepped inside the elevator just before the doors closed. "We'll give you a promotion and a five-thousand-dollar increase."

"No, thanks, sweetie. I love your suit. Congratulations, by the way. You look amazing."

"Tia, we need you. You're what we want. And with Chance gone for good, we can turn this station into something Atlanta viewers will be proud of for years to come. I can go higher. Five-thousand signing bonus, and another five-thousand raise."

Tia regarded Rhonda/Ronnie, not acknowledging how sweet the deal was. "I need to make this change and see what I'm made of."

"I'm not here to make it easy for you to leave. Twenty thousand, and three weeks vacation."

The elevator door opened on the first floor, and Tia stepped out.

She saw the squad car through the glass of the revolving doors, and her heart raced. She hadn't seen or heard from Byron since she'd left Judge Dunn's chambers on Monday.

Seeing his car made her salivate. She looked over her shoulder at Rhonda/Ronnie. "Wall office with a door, twenty-five-thousand raise. Seventy-five hundred signing bonus, separate and apart from the salary. Four weeks vacation a year."

"Deal," Ronnie said.

"And I want a lead slot."

Rhonda/Ronnie looked positively shocked. "I can't promise that. We're going to reshuffle, but—"

"Talk to Ben, and get back to me. What he has to say might surprise you."

Tia hurried out the door and felt crushing disappointment. The squad car didn't belong to Byron.

Chapter Twenty-five

Byron walked back into the squad room as a detective and felt nothing but pride. He'd paid his dues, and his hard work had paid off. He was finally, officially, a detective.

Heading to his old desk, he noticed Heather, the squad secretary, flapping papers to get his attention. "Detective, you have a guest."

"Heather, you can call me Byron."

"No, I can't," she said in a low voice as she turned him around and walked him away from her desk. "I'm training a new assistant, and she looks like she wants to make a couple of you a meal, if you know what I mean. From now on, you're Detective, and I'm Heather, and she's Ms. Ross, okay?"

Byron nodded. "Yes, ma'am. Where's my guest?"

"She's in conference room one."

"Who is she, and what does she want?" The idea of getting a case his first day with his gold shield excited him.

"Something about you owing her an apology."

Byron's hopes deflated. He'd probably trampled

her flowers or something. "Fine. I'll catch you later, Heather. Thanks."

"No problem, Byron," she whispered, and he grinned.

Taking a breath, he walked into the room.

"How can I—" Byron stopped when he saw it was Tia.

"Hey," she said, watching him.

"Hey. How are you?"

"Fine. I wanted to bring you something."

Byron sat in a rolling chair, leaving a chair between them.

Tia sure had changed. She wore a sexy cream-colored skirt with a sleeveless red blouse that tied at her waist. Her hair seemed longer since the last time he'd run his fingers through it, but he hadn't really been looking at her hair.

His eyes and his hands had been somewhere else.

She put a tiny red purse on the table, and he glanced at it.

She smiled at him. "That look says 'is it new?' The answer is no."

He sat back and chuckled. "It's you. Very cute."

"Thank you." Tia opened the purse and pulled out a check. Byron noted the folded paper as she slid it across the table to him.

"What's this?" he asked, not touching it.

"Repayment for my purses. I know you bought all of them. I just wanted to say thank you. You didn't have to do that."

"I know I didn't. And I'm not taking your money."

"Well, it's kind of a bribe. Maybe you can buy them back from Camilla."

"You know my sister?" Women amazed him. Then Byron remembered. "You talked to her the day you were at my house."

"I did. She's a nice lady." Tia's smile was quick, with a hint of melancholy. Was she feeling like he did, or did she want to give up on their relationship?

Byron looked at the check. Seventy-five hundred dollars. "Where'd you get the money?"

"I got a huge promotion, and that was my signing bonus."

"Tia, that's great news. I always knew you'd get back on your feet. What happened with your boss?"

"Chance was fired. Rhonda/Ronnie is in charge now."

"Your station will be number one in no time," Byron said, trying to think of a way to keep her there.

Tia closed her purse and pushed her chair back, standing.

"I won't take up any more of your time. I just wanted to say thank you for all you did for me. I know Judge Dunn didn't think much of your efforts, but you and I know what transpired between us. So, thanks, and good-bye."

"What transpired between us, Tia?" he asked, still sitting.

"We got really close. We needed each other, not just for the class, but individually. I needed you in my ear, even though I didn't want to hear some of the things you were saying."

"I needed you, too. Despite how I might have sounded, I admired you."

Her gaze met his, and she looked shocked. "Why?"

"Because you weren't scared of your emotions. You felt something, and right or wrong, you experienced it. You lived every moment until you decided to let that moment go. I was afraid to live. I had too many rules in my life. You weren't trying to live by any. I fell in love with that about you."

"You did?" she whispered.

"Yes, I did."

"And now?" she asked, her chocolate brown eyes watching him as he stood.

Byron saw himself falling deeper and let it happen. Soon he was against her body, her arms around his neck. Tia wouldn't let him kiss her or nuzzle her neck. She needed him to look into her eyes. "Do you still love me?" she asked him.

He braced his hands at her waist, holding her. "Yes. I love you very much."

"And what are you going to do about it?"

"Marry you, if you'll have me."

She was quiet for a few seconds. "Yes, love. I'll marry you."

Byron kissed Tia deeply for every moment he'd lain awake thinking about her, wondering if this moment would ever happen.

Many minutes later he still couldn't let her go.

Loving energy swirled around them, rocking the couple in a harmonious unity.

"Sweetheart," she said softly.

"Yes?"

"Can I have my check back?"

"Why?"

"I didn't know how else to approach you, so I came up with this. The check's no good. But I am."

He leaned back and looked down at her. "There's a penalty for writing detectives bad checks."

"What is it?"

"Unconditional love. Forever."

Tia peppered his face with sweet kisses. "I'm no fool. Sign me up."

Dear Readers:

I hope you enjoyed reading *What A Fool Believes*. This project was a lot of fun for me, and I'm thrilled that I had the opportunity to bring love and laughter into your reading world.

Please be sure to check out my Web site for the latest updates and information about my next novel, which will be my twentieth! In acknowledgment of this milestone, I'm kicking off a year-long celebration with contests, signings, and visits with readers' groups. In addition, one lucky reader will receive a signed bag of books, courtesy of Femme Fantastik, a group I cofounded with other wonderful authors. For more information, view my website at www.authorcarmengreen.com and femmefantastik.blogspot.com

Peace and Blessings,

Carmen Green